Do or Die

Donald Smith

PublishAmerica
Baltimore

First printing

ISBN: 1-4137-8213-2
PUBLISHED BY PUBLISHAMERICA, LLLP
www.publishamerica.com
Baltimore

Printed in the United States of America

For Betty

and our three sons

Don, Robert, and Rick

To brother Dick, the
best brother a brother
could have, with much
love and admiration,
Don

Chapter 1

Michael Donovan glanced up from the tax fraud file, startled by the sound of the door in the outer office banging against the wall.

He frowned and stepped out to see who it was. He was surprised to see a frightened-looking African-American girl standing there.

"Some men attacked me," she cried. "On the street outside they tried to force me into their car."

Donovan stared at her. "Attacked you?"

"Yes. Just seconds ago."

"Do you know who they were?"

She shook her head. "No. I've never seen them before."

Donovan didn't know why, but he felt as though he should know her. She was very pretty. And young. Not more than twenty.

"Have you any idea why they were trying to...to abduct you?" he asked.

"No, I don't." She hesitated. "I'd been shopping and had just come out of a store down the street. I walked to the corner and they pulled up in a car, jumped out, and grabbed me." She had control over her voice now.

"Did they see you come in here?"

"They saw me run into this building, I think." She glanced back toward the door. "I don't think they followed me." She wet her lips. She looked embarrassed. "I never ran so hard in all my life. I'm still trembling."

"Why don't you sit down?" Donovan motioned toward the chairs along the wall.

"No. No, thank you."

"Maybe they're still out there," he said. "Let's take a look from my office. You can get a good view of the street from there."

They stood by the window, and looked through the Venetian blind. Colorado Boulevard was lined with cars and the sidewalk crowded with shoppers rushing to take advantage of after-Christmas sales.

"See them?...Or their car?" he asked.

She stared down at the crowded sidewalk. "No," she said. She sighed. "I think they've probably gone by now." She turned toward him with a wry look, her small gold earrings, shaped like rosebuds, glinting in the light from the window.

"Can you think of any reason anyone would want to kidnap you?" he asked as they walked back to the outer office.

She shook her head. "No...no, I can't."

"How many men were there?"

"I don't know. Two of them jumped out of the car."

"Were they blacks?"

She frowned. "No. They were whites."

He stopped and faced her, wishing there were some way he could help her.

"Do you know what kind of car they were driving?"

She shrugged. "No, I don't. It could've been a Buick or Chevy—about that size and style. It was dark red, I think. It all happened so fast, I'm not sure of anything."

"I think I'd better call the police," he said.

Her eyes narrowed. "I...I don't see what good it would do. It would be impossible to catch them now."

"I still think the police should know," he persisted.

"I'd really rather not get involved with them," she said." I think it would be a waste of their time." She tried to smile. "But thanks, anyway. And thanks, too, for being so nice about my barging in like this." She paused. "I guess I'd better go now."

"Are you driving?" He still couldn't shake the feeling he'd seen her somewhere before.

"Yes. I'm parked a little way down the street."

"I'll walk you to your car."

"Oh, will you?" She looked relieved.

"Yes, I'd be glad to."

"Well, that's very nice of you."

Suddenly he realized why she looked so familiar. "I should've known," he exclaimed with a wry, apologetic smile. "Your picture's been everywhere. You're the Rose Queen, aren't you?"

She hesitated, then nodded. "Yes," she said. "I'm Carlene Edwards."

He held out his hand. "I'm Michael Donovan. It's a shame we had to meet like this."

She shook his hand with a rueful expression. "That's why I was worried about calling the police. I don't think it's the kind of publicity the Tournament of Roses officials would like."

"You don't suppose the fact that you *are* the Rose Queen has something to do with what happened to you, do you?"

She shook her head. "I don't see why."

He didn't want to tell her that her being black might have something to do with it, what with so much racial hatred still existing in the country.

He put his hand on the doorknob. "Let me check the hall before you step out."

The hall was empty except for a man and a woman standing together down at the far end of it. He didn't recognize either of them, and they didn't appear to notice him.

He motioned to her to step out, and locked the door behind them. Then, taking her elbow, he guided her down to the street below.

"Which way?" he asked.

She pointed to their right. "Down the block and around the corner on El Molino."

Still holding her elbow, he guided her down the crowded sidewalk, half expecting to be confronted by the men who had tried to kidnap her.

When they reached the corner of El Molino, she paused and pointed at her car, a white Honda Civic coupe. It was parked about sixty feet down from them on their side of the street.

"That's it," she said. "The little white Honda."

He took her by the elbow again and they started down toward her car.

"By the way," he said, "where are you going from here?"

She gave him a grim little smile. "After all this, straight home. And as fast as I can without breaking any speed limits."

"Keep your doors locked, and watch your rearview mirror," he warned her. "And if you see anybody following you, step on the gas and get out of there as fast as you can. Find a police station or police car. Or find a service station or someplace you can drive in to and get help."

She nodded. "I will," she said.

They stopped beside her car, and she held out her hand and started to thank him. Suddenly he felt something hard jab into the middle of his back.

"Don't move!" someone said in a harsh voice.

He stiffened and glanced back over his shoulder. Two men stood there, hard-faced and menacing looking. The red-haired man had gripped Carlene Edwards' arms against her sides, and the black-bearded man was jamming a handgun up against Michael's back.

Michael felt a rush of anger. "What the hell do you think you're doing?" he cried.

The two men ignored him.

A dark red four-door sedan drew up alongside Carlene Edwards' Honda.

"Okay," the black-bearded man said. He jabbed Michael's back again. Hard. "Get over there, next to that building."

"The girl," Michael said. "Leave her alone. I'll..."

"Get over there!" the black-bearded man growled.

"You dirty bastard!" Michael cried. He spun around and swung his fist at the bearded man's chin. The man dodged and slammed his gun barrel down across the side of Michael's head.

Michael staggered back against the girl's car, his eyes blurring with pain. As if through a mist, he saw the red-haired man wrestling Carlene Edwards into the backseat of the dark red car. He tried to straighten up. The black-bearded man shoved him back against the car with one hand and slammed his gun barrel against the side of Michael's head with the other. Michael sagged and fell to his knees.

He shook his head and tried to get up, but couldn't. He swore to himself in frustration. The car was carrying Carlene Edwards away and he wasn't stopping it; wasn't even getting its license number.

He gritted his teeth, forced himself to his feet. He had to get to a phone, inform the police.

He started up the sidewalk toward Colorado Boulevard. An elderly couple coming toward him looked at him in a strange way, then quickened their steps and made a wide path around him.

He reached up and touched his head above his right ear. His fingers came away sticky with blood.

Chapter 2

Dottie Hunter was unlocking the door when he got back to their office.

"My God!" she cried, glancing up at him. "What's happened to you, Michael?" Her face looked as white as her hair. "Your head's bleeding!"

"Let's get inside," he said, pushing the door open.

"I'll call a doctor," she said.

"Forget the doctor," he said. "Call the police."

"The police?" Her blue eyes looked scared behind her rimless glasses.

"Yes, the police. I'll talk to them in my office."

She hesitated. "You sure you're okay?"

"Make the call, Dottie. It's an emergency."

She started for her desk and Michael went into his office, sick over what had happened to the girl. Who the hell were those bastards anyway? And what the hell were they up to?

As he dabbed at the blood above his ear with his handkerchief, his phone rang. It was Dottie.

"Lieutenant Ferraro of the Pasadena Police Department is on the phone," she said.

"Thanks, Dottie." Michael's hand tightened on the receiver. He identified himself to the lieutenant and explained where his offices were. Then, in as few words as possible, he described his encounter with the Rose Queen and the two thugs.

The lieutenant asked several questions in a calm, careful voice, then said, "I'd like to talk to you in your office, if it's all right. I'll bring a member of the department who's experienced in these matters with me. We can be there in fifteen minutes."

"Fine," said Michael.

"Be sure to keep this to yourself," the lieutenant cautioned him. "We don't want the news media getting wind of this until we're ready for them."

"All right," Michael said. "I'll leave all that up to you."

He put the receiver back in place and stepped into the outer office. He knew Dottie would be bursting with curiosity about what had happened to him. She wouldn't let him say a word, though, until she had examined the gash above his ear. Then, satisfied that he wasn't going to bleed to death right then and there, she asked him to tell her what had happened when she left to go to the post office.

She was shocked at what he told her. "Why, they might've killed you!" she cried, her eyes glinting with concern. "And that poor girl! What in the world do they want her for?"

She pushed her glasses back against the bridge of her nose, peering at him with worried eyes.

"I still think you'd better have a doctor look at your head, Michael. You might've had a concussion."

"Now, Dottie."

"I mean it, Michael. You look awfully pale."

He patted her shoulder. "I'm all right, believe me."

She sighed. "Well, I know one thing for sure. I know you'd better take it easy the rest of the day."

He gave her a faint smile. "I plan to," he said.

But take it easy, he couldn't. He had to finish work on the Kenworthy tax fraud brief, and it was rather technical and complicated. So he forced himself to put Carlene Edwards out of his mind and got right to work.

Twenty minutes later, Dottie rang to inform him that a Lt. Ferraro and a Sgt. Wren were there to see him. Michael met them at the door and ushered them in. Lt. Ferraro was a thin, balding man in a plain gray suit, and Sgt. Wren was a square-jawed man in a brown sport coat and tan slacks.

"Please sit down," Michael said, indicating the chairs across from him. He waited for them to sit down, then sat down himself.

Lt. Ferraro reached inside his suit coat, took out a notebook and a ballpoint pen, then leaned back and said, "Mind telling us again what the girl told you when she entered your office? And then what happened when the two men assaulted you?"

When Michael finished, Lt. Ferraro asked him to describe the two men again. Michael repeated what he'd told him earlier over the phone.

"The man who forced the girl into the car was about six feet tall and had red hair," he said. "The man who bashed me over the head was two or three inches taller than I am, and I'm about an inch over six feet. He had a black beard, cut short, and a deep voice."

"How were they dressed?"

Michael shrugged. "I'm not sure. I think they were wearing suits and ties, though."

The lieutenant jotted something down in his notebook. "Anything else you can think of or remember? Did they speak with accents? Did they have distinguishing marks on their faces? Scars, birthmarks...anything like that?"

Michael shook his head. "I think I've told you everything."

"On the phone, you said you thought their car might be a Buick. Do you still think so?"

"I don't know. I'm not sure. It might've been, but...Sorry, I'm just not sure. All I know is, it was dark red and was a four-door sedan."

"But you still don't remember anything about the license plate? Whether it was a California plate or an out-of-state plate?"

"No, I don't. As I told you before, the car was gone by the time I could get to my feet."

The lieutenant turned to Sgt. Wren. "Anything you'd like to ask Mr. Donovan?"

The sergeant tugged at one earlobe. "I'm just a bit puzzled about the fact that the girl ran all the way up here to your office to look for help. Why come all the way up here? Why didn't she run into one of the offices on the first floor?"

"I don't know," Michael said. "But the first thing you see when you come in off the street is the stairs. They're right there in front of you. I guess she did what anybody who was running away from someone would do. She ran right up them and into the first door she came to."

Lt. Ferraro leaned back in the chair, eying Michael with a quizzical expression.

"Here's a different kind of question for you, Mr. Donovan. Why do you think the girl was abducted?"

Michael hesitated. "I don't know," he said. He pushed his penholder to one side. "Whoever those two men are, though, they're either very stupid or very daring to do what they did, in broad daylight, with the streets crowded the way they are."

Lt. Ferraro rubbed his cheek. "That's an interesting point, Mr. Donovan. It does seem a poor time and place to abduct someone, doesn't it?" He paused. "Incidentally, I've asked one of our men to get in touch with you as soon as he can. He's an artist and his name is Jack Josephson. He'll ask you to describe the two men, then he'll make a composite of each one of them. You should be hearing from him any time now." He looked at Sgt. Wren. "Anything else you can think of, Sergeant?"

The sergeant shook his head. "I think we've covered every thing."

Lt. Ferraro and Sgt. Wren got up, and Lt. Ferraro took a card out of his billfold and handed it to Michael.

"My office and home phone numbers are on that," he said. "If you think of anything you think I should know...even though it might not seem too important...don't hesitate to call me, night or day."

Chapter 3

Norm Carlson got back from LA a little before five. He knocked on Michael's door and called out, "Hey, you, in there. It's God's gift to jurisprudence is back from Sin City! You busy?"

Michael smiled and put down his pencil, glad to have a break. "Come in, Norm."

The door opened and his partner, Norm Carlson, stepped in, tall and lanky, attaché case in hand.

"What's all this Dottie's been telling me?" he asked with a quizzical expression. "I'm surprised to see you're still alive."

Michael gave him a knowing look. "So she's told you about it, has she?"

"Yup." Norm dropped into the chair opposite Michael's desk and put his attaché case down on the floor beside him. Then he took off his glasses and looked across at Michael with a sympathetic little smile.

"Sounds as though you had a pretty tough time of it, pardner," he said.

Michael grimaced. "It's certainly not one of the best days of my life."

Norm rubbed his eyes for a moment, then put his glasses back on, his shrewd brown eyes glinting.

"Dottie said you got a nasty gash on your head." He paused. "Looks as though you're developing a big bump up there, too."

"Feels like it," Michael said. He reached up and touched the swollen area above his ear.

"Think you'd better see a doc? Dottie says you might've had a concussion."

"I'm fine, Norm."

Norm sighed and shook his head. "That's what Dottie said you'd say...as if I didn't know better." He leaned back and crossed his long legs. "How about giving me a quick rundown on what happened...just in case Dottie left something out?"

Michael told him what he'd told Dottie, and then summarized what the lieutenant and the sergeant had had to say.

"So here I am," he finished, "bloody but unbowed."

Norm gave him a wry look. "Who do you suppose did it, Mike? You don't suppose it could be some of those racist nuts we were talking about the other day, do you?...The ones upset about having a black Rose Queen."

Michael shrugged. "I don't know, Norm. Anything's possible with the world all topsy-turvy the way it is now."

"Dottie said you had some guy in here a little while ago drawing pictures from your description of the guys who kidnapped the girl."

Michael nodded. "I got only a quick look at them, so I don't think I helped him very much."

Norm glanced at his watch. "You've been a badly abused lad. How about closing up and joining Ruth and me for a little libation at Charlie's? It'll probably do you some good to relax a bit after what you've been through." He picked up his attaché case and got to his feet.

"You going right over?"

"Yup. Told Ruth I'd meet her there at five-thirty. She told me to be sure to ask you and Dottie to join us."

"I could use a good stiff drink or two," Michael said. "Tell you what, I'll finish up this thing I'm working on, and see you there in half and hour or so."

"Great," said Norm. "If you promise to behave yourself, I'll even let you buy me a drink."

Michael made several more corrections on the material he was working on, then went out to tell Dottie that he hoped to have everything done for her by noon tomorrow.

"I'll reserve part of the afternoon for it, then," she said. She wrote something down on her memo pad, then looked up at him. "Norm says you're going to join him and Ruth at Charlie's in a little while."

He nodded. "I'm headed there now. You're going to join us, aren't you?"

She shook her head. "Wish I could. But Bill just called...just a minute ago, in fact. He wants me to drive him to Alhambra to pick up the van. He had the brakes relined at a garage there, and it's ready to go."

"Well," said Michael, "sorry you can't join us."

"So am I. Michael. Tell Norm and Ruth why I can't make it, won't you?"

"Will do. Say hello to Bill for me."

"All right, Michael...Oh, before you go, I have these insurance forms typed up. All they need is your signature."

Michael put down his attaché case, then bent and signed the forms with the pen she had handed him.

"Better not stay too long at Charlie's." she cautioned him, taking back the pen. "You had a pretty hard blow to the head, you know."

He nodded. "I won't stay very long. See you tomorrow, Dottie."

"Good night, Michael."

He left the building and walked to the parking garage out back. His Chevy Cavalier, a bright and perky red sedan, stood out from all the other cars on the first level. He locked his attaché case in the trunk, then climbed behind the steering wheel, started the engine, and pushed the Sinatra cassette into the tape deck. Sinatra was halfway through "Come Fly With Me," his voice warm and sure. It was sad to know he was gone now—as was most of his kind of music.

As Michael drove out the exit he saw a man and a woman standing by a car parked at the curb. The man glanced his way, then turned and said something to the woman. It took Michael a second or two to realize who they were. They were the same two persons who had been standing at the end of the hall when he and Carlene Edwards left his office.

He drove on past them, wondering who they were.

Chapter 4

There were several persons at the bar when he walked in the backdoor of Charlie's. He said hello to Dave, the bartender, and Dave told him that Norm and Ruth were waiting for him down near the fireplace.

He stepped down into the main room, which had oak-paneled walls and brass fixtures and subdued lighting. Norm and Ruth were sitting at a small table next to the fireplace. Norm saw him and waved and Michael went on down and bent and kissed Ruth on the cheek.

"You've had some day, haven't you?" she said, her dark eyes big with concern. Norm told me what happened."

"It was a bit unusual," he said, sitting down across from them with a wry smile.

"I think it's absolutely horrible," she exclaimed. "Did you know I know that girl? She's taken a couple of classes from me, and I'm her faculty adviser."

"I think you did mention it when she was chosen Rose Queen," he said.

"She's really a very nice girl, and exceptionally bright and talented."

"I got that impression."

"I pray to God she isn't harmed and they'll let her go."

"We all do, Ruth."

She leaned forward, peering at the spot above his ear where the black-bearded thug had slugged him with his gun.

"That monster must've hit you awfully hard, Mike. That's quite a bump you've got there."

"I'll survive," he smiled.

Norm put his hand on his wife's shoulder. "I think Mike would probably rather talk about something else, honey."

Ruth nodded, her eyes softening. "Sorry, Mike."

Michael smiled at her. "There's nothing to be sorry about, Ruth."

"By the way, Mike," Norm said, "I meant to tell you when I got back from LA. Someone broke into our house yesterday while Ruth and I were gone. Whoever it was walked off with three of my guns."

"No fooling!" Michael was surprised.

"Yeah. Broke the glass and took them right out of the cabinet. A couple of my Smith and Wessons. One I particularly liked...that .357 Magnum. You know the one. And another favorite of mine, a Colt Goldcup .45."

"How in the world did they get in?"

"Through a side window in the family room. Broke it and climbed right in."

"It's revolting. Did they take anything else?"

"No, I don't think so. Nothing else seems to be missing, fortunately."

"Strange they would take only the guns. And only three of them, at that."

"Yeah, I know. But there's not much else of value around the place."

Michael frowned. You reported it to the police, didn't you?"

"Oh, sure. Right away." Norm shrugged. "But enough about that. We're here to relax and..."

Ruth put her hand on Norm's arm. "Here's the girl to take our order."

Norm and Ruth ordered another round of martinis, and Michael ordered a vodka gimlet on the rocks.

"Oh, I forgot to tell you," Michael said after the waitress left, "Dottie can't make it. Bill called her at the last minute and wanted her to drive him to Alhambra to pick up their van. He had the brakes relined."

Ruth looked disappointed then her face brightened. "By the way, Mike, I saw Ellen last night at an AAUW meeting. She looked just wonderful. She asked about you, of course. Said to give you her love. Said to tell you to call her for lunch sometime."

Michael tried not to show his feelings. He and Ellen had ended their marriage by mutual consent a little over a year ago. They'd soon learned that two lawyers in one family were one too many. But the sad thing was, he missed her terribly. Couldn't get over her, in fact.

He managed to smile at Ruth. "Thanks for the message," he said. "It's a shame, but I rarely see Ellen anymore. You'd think we'd run into each other more often, but we don't."

Ruth nodded. "I know. Pasadena's become a little city now. I guess you could go for years without accidentally running into someone you know."

"And that ain't all bad, either," Norm said.

"Cynic!" Ruth said.

Norm laughed good-naturedly. "I read somewhere that a cynic sees things as they are, not as they ought to be.... Who said that, anyway, Mike? Was it Mencken?"

"I don't think so," said Michael. "I think it was Ambrose Bierce."

"Ambrose Bierce?"

"Yes, I think so."

"But who the devil is Ambrose Bierce?"

"He was a journalist, a writer. Wrote all kinds of things...essays, stories, books. He was quite brilliant, I guess. When he was about seventy he disappeared into Mexico and was never heard from again."

Norm peered at Ruth over the top of his glasses, which had slipped halfway down his nose.

"See," he said. "I've been telling you this for years. This guy, this unassuming Irishman, Michael Clancy Donovan, Jr., is a virtual compendium of everything in this crazy world of ours that's quite useless."

They laughed and ordered another round of drinks, and shortly after that, Jan Ashby came walking toward them. She was slim and blonde and attractive, and she played and sang the kind of songs Michael liked—the best of the old as well as the best of the new.

She smiled and stopped at their table, looking chic in a simple, form-fitting black dress. Michael got up and asked her to join them.

"Thanks, but I can't," she said. "I just wanted to say hello…Good heavens, Mike! What happened to your head?"

"It's nothing," he said. "Just a little bump."

"It doesn't look very little to me."

He smiled. "It's nothing' to be concerned about."

"Well, if you say so." She didn't look convinced. "Well, as I was going to say"—her glance took in Norm and Ruth—"I just wanted to say hello and ask if there's anything you'd like me to play for you."

Michael looked at Ruth and Norm. "Any requests?"

Ruth smiled and looked at Norm. "I'll let Norm choose."

"How about 'People'," Norm said. "I know you like it."

"I love it," Ruth said.

Jan turned to Michael with a knowing smile. "I suppose you want the usual…anything by Cole Porter or George Gershwin."

He smiled and nodded.

"Well," she said, "I'd better get going. The room's starting to fill up already." She flashed them a bright smile. "Have a nice time," she said. "If you think of anything else you'd like to hear, just let me know."

It was close to seven-thirty when they got ready to leave Charlie's.

"Why don't you come home with us and have dinner?" Ruth said to Michael as the three of them stood up. "It won't take any time at all to broil some steaks."

"Good idea," said Norm. He patted Michael's back. "You look as though you could use a few good home-cooked meals, old friend."

Michael gave both of them a grateful smile. "Thanks," he said. "It's sweet of you to offer, but I'd better get home and work on some tax papers I promised to get to Dottie by noon tomorrow."

As they turned to go, Jan Ashby called across to Michael from the piano.

"May I see you a second, Mike?"

Michael nodded, wondering what she wanted. "I won't be long," he said to Norm and Ruth. "You go ahead. I'll meet you at the backdoor."

He crossed over to Jan, still wondering what she wanted.

"Thanks for sending over the drink," she said, putting her hand on his arm and looking up at him with a warm smile.

"You're welcome, Jan. Thanks for the great music."

She hesitated. "We should get together sometime, Mike...somewhere other than here at Charlie's. I'm sure we'd have lots to talk about. And we're both unencumbered, so to speak...both free spirits."

"I know."

"So let's do get together."

"We'll have to do that, Jan."

"I mean soon."

"All right."

"Is that a promise, Mike?"

"It's a promise," he said. He felt guilty because he didn't mean it, because, even though the prospect of starting a relationship with her was tempting, he didn't want to become involved with her in a serious way. Or with anybody else, for that matter. Not now. Not, at least, until he could put Ellen out of his mind, once and for all.

He said good night to her and joined Norm and Ruth at the backdoor, where they stood waiting for him.

"Better be careful, Mike," Ruth warned, squinting at him with shrewd, perceptive eyes. "Jan has had her eyes set on you ever since you and Ellen broke up. If not before."

"We're just friends, Ruth," he protested.

"Don't kid yourself, Mike. She thinks you're the catch of the century."

The parking lot lights were on when they stepped outside, and the parking lot was jammed with cars. They walked down toward where they were parked, talking casually.

Suddenly Michael stopped and stared, stunned, at his car. In big bold letters were the words *NIGGER LOVER*. They were sprayed in white paint all the way across the top of his windshield, and just below them were the words *THE ROSE QUEEN IS A SLUT*.

"My God!" Norm exclaimed. "Look at that!"

Chapter 5

MICHAEL CLENCHED HIS FISTS. It was obvious now. Racist lunatics had kidnapped Carlene Edwards.

Norm put his hand on Michael's shoulder. "We'd better call the police, Mike."

Michael tried to control his anger. "I don't think it would do any good," he said. "There isn't much to look at. Or much that can be done. I'll call Lieutenant Ferraro first thing in the morning. "

"I think we'd better call them now," Norm insisted. "Someone ought to come out here and take a look at this. Who knows what they might find? They might even find something that could lead them to the kidnappers."

Michael looked at the obscenities on his windshield. Maybe Norm was right. They might pick up some fingerprints...or they might find a paint can in the area that could be traced.

"All right," he said. "I'll call them."

They went back into Charlie's to make the call. Michael didn't want to bother Lt. Ferraro at his home, so he called the police department instead. He was told a police car would be right out. They went back out and waited next to his car for the police to come.

Within a few minutes, a police car pulled into the parking lot next to them and two uniformed police officers got out.

"One of you Michael Donovan?" one of the officers asked.

"Yes," Michael said, stepping forward. "That's my car there. You can see what they did to it."

The officer, who had a black mustache, nodded. "The dispatcher said you identified yourself as the lawyer who tried to help the Rose Queen when she was kidnapped."

"That's right," Michael said.

"Well, let's see if we can find anything around here that might help us tell who did it."

He and the other officer, who was clean-shaven, checked the windshield of Michael's car, looking for fingerprints. Then they walked all the way around the car, peering under it with their flashlights.

"Didn't have any luck finding prints on the windshield," the clean-shaven officer said, coming back toward them. "But the paint can might be somewhere around here."

While Michael, Ruth and Norm stood there waiting, the two officers probed the shadows in the surrounding area with their flashlights. They then moved out as far as the brick wall at the end of the parking lot and checked the trash barrels there.

When they came back, they were sober-faced.

"We didn't find anything," the officer with the mustache said. "But we'll go ahead and file a report. We'll need your driver's license and your vehicle registration. It's just routine."

Michael handed the officer his driver's license, then got the vehicle registration form out of his glove compartment. The officer write down the information he needed, then handed the driver's license and registration form back to Michael.

"Thank you, Mr. Donovan," he said. "Sorry about the mess they made on your windshield."

Michael shrugged. "Could've been worse, I guess." He paused. "Will Lieutenant Ferraro be told about this? I promised to keep him informed if anything related to the kidnapping came up."

"Yes, he'll be notified."

"Well, thanks very much for coming out," Michael said. "Sorry you didn't find something that would help."

"Oh, we might get them yet," the clean-shaven officer said. "In fact, we probably will."

As the two officers got back in their car, Michael turned to Norm and Ruth.

"You two might as well run along," he said. "I'll try to get some of that stuff off the windshield before I take off."

"I'll help you," said Norm.

"No, thanks." Michael said. "I can manage."

"I insist, Mike."

"Really, Norm. I can take care of it. You two run along."

Michael's apartment was in a large complex on South Madison. He'd moved there after he and Ellen had separated and filed for divorce. He pulled into the driveway, inserted his plastic card in the metal box on the post, and waited for the garage door to open. Then he drove on down the ramp and into the basement parking area and parked in the space reserved for him.

Getting his attaché case out of the trunk, he took the elevator to the lobby. He got his mail out of his mailbox and the morning edition of the *Los Angeles Times* off the table in the corner. And then he took the elevator on up to his apartment on the third floor.

Although he wasn't at all hungry, he made and ate a toasted cheese sandwich and drank a glass of milk. Then he glanced through the first few pages of the *Times,* half expecting to see something on the kidnapping. He knew it was impossible, though, since it was the morning edition, and the kidnapping hadn't occurred until later that day.

After he looked through his mail, he was tempted to turn on the TV to see whether the police had broken the news yet about the kidnapping. But he decided against it. Better get his work done first, and catch the news later.

He went into the den, took the Kenworthy file out of his attaché case, then sat down at his desk with his portable tape recorder. After he had dictated several changes in the brief, he made some additions to it. Then he went through all the depositions and related material he had in the file.

He worked without stopping for close to two hours when the phone suddenly rang.

"Michael Donovan speaking," he said, picking up the receiver.

"Are you the attorney?" someone asked in a deep, masculine voice.

Michael hesitated. "I'm an attorney, yes."

"And you have a partner named Carlson?" The voice somehow seemed familiar.

"Yes, I do. How can I help you?"

There was a burst of laughter. "How d'you like the paint job we did on your car, Donovan?"

Michael gripped the receiver. He knew the voice now. It was the voice of the black-bearded man who had bashed him over the head with his gun—one of the kidnappers.

"You shouldn't have gotten yourself involved with the nigger girl, Donovan," the man said.

Michael struggled to be calm. "I don't know what you mean."

"You shouldn't have tried to help her, man. That's what I mean. Why, it's an insult to every white woman in the country to have a female nigger made queen of the Tournament of Roses. And it's an insult to all us white men, too. And we're going to let the whole damned country know what a lousy mistake it was." The man paused, and his voice took on a crafty tone. "By the way, Counselor, don't go getting cute and get somebody there with you to get to another phone and try to trace this call. It won't do any good, you know."

Michael's heart thudded against his chest. "Where's the girl?" he said. "What've you done with her?"

The man snorted. "Forget that little black slut! I didn't call to spend all my time talking about her. I got other things to talk about. What I want to know is what did the cops say about that paint job on your car? We watched you talk to them, y'know. You'd never guess how close we were. In fact, we were parked in a car only a short distance away from you. With the windows down, we could almost hear what you were saying."

Michael clenched his teeth, tried to control his emotions.

The man laughed. "You might not think so, but we're glad you called them. The cops, I mean. We wanted them to know. In fact, we want the newspapers and TV and everybody in the whole damned country to know. That's the reason we kidnapped the little slut in broad daylight...right out in front of everybody...right in the middle of downtown Pasadena."

The man paused and cleared his throat. "But that isn't all," he continued, "my friends and I are going to take care of another big job very soon now, and I guarantee it'll make mighty big news. It'll make every nigger in this country know goddamned well they're not wanted or safe here anymore. And that goes for all the slant-eyed and brown-skinned vermin and the money-grubbing Jews, too. We're going to get rid of all of them. We're going to make a mighty big news story, all right. I guarantee it. Just wait and..."

Michael's stomach cramped. "You're crazy!" he blurted. "What you're saying is insane!"

"Insane!" the man snorted. "Listen, shyster, what's going on in this country is what's insane. Letting these stinking leftist liberals take over everything...the government, the movies ...newspapers...TV...You name it. Letting them turn us into a stinking socialist welfare state. But we're going to change all that. We're going to save this country for the' white people, for God-fearing people who..."

Michael's head had begun to ache in a dull, heavy way. The man's voice had risen and he was almost shouting now, and lacing what he had to say with obscenities. It was more than

Michael could take. He slammed down the receiver, sickened by what the man had said. For a moment he stood there uncertainly, feeling the sweat sliding down his sides.

He doubted that it would do any good to try to have the call traced. The man was probably calling from a phone booth somewhere. And it wouldn't do any good to call the police now or call Lt. Ferraro at his home. It was awfully late, and what could they do? About the only thing he could do, he supposed, was call Lt. Ferraro in the morning.

He got up, his head still reeling from the phone call, and started clearing off his desk. The man was obviously psychotic. What he'd said was wholly irrational. Demented. Paranoid. And he was obviously dangerous. It scared Michael to think of what he and his cohorts might do to Carlene Edwards...what they might have done to her already. And what had that lunatic meant when he said they "were going to do another big job very soon?"

What kind of sick craziness did they have in mind, anyway?

Michael rubbed his eyes. His head was still reeling, pulsing painfully. What he needed now was a long, hot, relaxing shower. He went into the bathroom, took a couple of aspirins, and got into the shower. For a long time he stood there, letting the hot water cascade down over his neck and back, trying to block out of his mind everything about the kidnapping and the call he'd just received.

When he got out, he felt better. He dried himself and went into the bedroom to get some clean pajamas. He pulled out the bottom drawer of the dresser and took out the top pair of pajamas. As he did so, he saw Ellen's photograph sticking out from the bottom of the pile where he'd stuck it a couple of weeks ago. He pulled it on out, put it on the top of the dresser and stood there looking at it.

Ellen seemed to be looking back at him with a loving smile. He looked at her intelligent, self-assured face, her dark-brown eyes, her nicely molded, expressive mouth, her lovely dark hair, and he wondered, with a twinge of regret, whether she kept a photograph of him somewhere in that apartment of hers over on Euclid Avenue. He shrugged and put her photograph back in the dresser drawer under the other pajamas.

What was that old saying?...Out of sight, out of mind?

CHAPTER 6

SHORTLY AFTER SEVEN-THIRTY THE NEXT MORNING, while finishing a second cup of coffee, he heard the bad news on the radio:

"The big story this morning," the newscaster was saying, "concerns the kidnapping early yesterday afternoon in downtown Pasadena of the Tournament of Roses Queen, eighteen-year-old Carlene Edwards. In an act apparently related to the kidnapping, Edwards' married sister's car was firebombed and destroyed late last night at the home of their widowed mother at 1204 Clayton Street in Pasadena.

"Firemen called to the scene of the firebombing," the newscaster went on, "found the 1996 Toyota Camry gutted in the driveway. A man who identified himself as a member of the White Unity organization telephoned the *Los Angeles Times* only minutes after the firebombing to claim credit for kidnapping young Edwards and firebombing her sister's car. White Unity is a radical organization of white supremacists now operating throughout the United States.

"A spokesperson for the Pasadena Police Department stated that several militia movements in the country are believed to support the White Unity movement and are..."

There was more, but Michael, sickened by what he'd already heard, got up and turned off the radio. *The bastards! The dirty bastards! So kidnapping the girl wasn't enough for them? They had to attack her sister, too!*

Feeling depressed, he got his attaché case and left the apartment. On the way to his office, he stopped by the Chevrolet garage to see about getting the painted obscenities taken off his car. He was told that if he left his car there it could be done by five o'clock that afternoon. In the meantime, he would be provided with a loaner.

When he got to his office a few minutes later, Dottie looked at him with .an indignant expression on her usually pleasant face.

"Norm told me about the rotten thing they did to your car last night," she exclaimed.

Michael shrugged. "That's why I'm a bit late. I left the car at the Chevrolet garage to have the paint taken off. Not only was there paint allover the windshield, there was some on the hood, too. Anyway, they gave me a loaner to drive for the rest of the day. And I can pick up my car after five."

"Well, that's good. It's a darned shame what they did, and all because you tried to help that poor girl." She squinted up at him through her glasses. "I suppose you got the news about what they did to her sister's car."

Michael nodded. "I'm afraid so."

"It's really scary, Michael. First, the kidnapping. And then what they did to your car. And then this firebombing. Evidently there's some kind of tie-in between this crazy White Unity movement and the militias. Sounds like the start of a race war or something, doesn't it?"

"It doesn't sound very good. Where's Norm? Does he know about the firebombing?"

"Yes, he does. He's really disgusted." She nodded toward Norm's door. "He's in his office now with a client." She paused, her expression softening. "Your head looks much better this morning, Michael. Looks like most of the swelling's gone."

"It feels better," he said. "By the way, I worked on the Kenworthy file last night and should finish it up this morning. I should have it ready for you by one."

"All right, Michael."

"Well, I'd better get to work," he said. He started toward his office.

"Oh," she said, "I meant to tell you, Michael. You've had a couple of phone calls already this morning. I left the slips on your desk."

"Thanks, Dottie." He went on into his office and adjusted the Venetian blinds to let some sunlight in. Then he sat down and looked at the call slips on his desk. One was from Lt. Ferraro. The other, he was surprised to see, was from Ellen.

Lt. Ferraro had asked that he call him back as soon as possible. Michael did so immediately, and the lieutenant answered on the first ring.

"I suppose you know we released the report on the kidnapping to the news media last night," the lieutenant said.

"Yes, I know."

"Then you probably know about the firebombing of her sister's car."

"Yes, I heard about it on the news this morning. It's revolting."

"Sorry to learn what they did to your car. I got the report this morning."

Michael frowned. "They'll do anything, I guess...anything to push their cause." He hesitated. "Have you heard from them yet?"

"No, we haven't. But if that caller to the *Times* last night wasn't a crackpot, at least we know who they are now, who we're dealing with."

Michael told him then about the phone call he'd received last night from the black-bearded thug.

"They're very sick people," the lieutenant said when he finished.

"And dangerous," Michael said.

"No doubt about it," agreed the lieutenant. "I think you'll be glad to know we've got the cooperation of the FBI on this, which should help a great deal. And that's one of the reasons I wanted to talk to you. One of their agents should get in touch with you sometime today, I believe. And another thing, in order to keep the news hawks from bothering us all day, we've called a news conference for ten this morning. It means our media representative will have to give them your name and explain how you figure into all this. And that means when we're through here, they'll probably come hightailing over to your place to get your account of the kidnapping. So you better be prepared. They'll probably be descending on you en masse. Cameras and all."

Michael thanked him for the warning and for keeping him informed and then said goodbye. And then he leaned forward and picked up the other call slip. In her fine, precise script, Dottie had written, "Ellen wants you to call her at her office sometime this morning if you can."

He glanced at his watch. Nine-twenty. He picked up the receiver, and in only a matter of seconds was giving his name to Ellen's secretary.

A moment later, Ellen's voice rose warmly in his ear.

"Hello, Mike," she said. "Thanks for returning my call. Are you all right?"

"Why, of course, Ellen. I' m fine." His throat tightened. Just hearing her voice could do that to him.

"I've been worried about you," she said. "Ruth Carlson tried to get in touch with me last night to tell me about your dreadful experience with the kidnappers, but I was out. She called again this morning before I left for work and told me all about it...also about their firebombing that girl's sister's car. I was in a hurry this morning and didn't read or hear the news, so it all came as quite a shock. Ruth said not to worry, though. She said you have a bad cut on your head but otherwise you're all right."

"As I said, Ellen, I'm just fine." He felt like a damned fool, sounding so stiff, so formal. "It's nice of you to be concerned," he added lamely.

"You know I am, Mike." There was a slight note of hurt in her voice. "Anyhow, it's all so incredible. I bet it's been awfully hectic for you, hasn't it?"

"A little hectic, I guess."

"Have the reporters gotten to you yet?"

"Funny you should ask. I just talked with someone from the Pasadena Police Department. He said they're meeting with reporters at ten this morning, and that they'd all probably come running over here to question me about the kidnapping."

"Bet you don't look forward to that."

"No, I don't."

"Well, Mike, I've got a client coming in any second now, so I'd better get right to the point. The main reason I called was to ask whether you'd care to have a drink with me after work this afternoon. It would give us a chance to relax and chat for a little while. You can tell me everything that happened yesterday...about the kidnapping, I mean. Are you free to get together?"

He was surprised that she wanted to see him. "Yes, I think so," he said, not wanting to sound too eager.

"Good. Where would you like to meet...at Charlie's?"

"That would be fine."

"Say five-thirty?"

"Five-thirty it is."

"Good luck with the Fourth Estate."

"Thanks. I'll need it."

He put the receiver back in place and sat there a few seconds, wondering why she wanted to see him. The last time she'd called him was about three months ago. She'd called then to ask his opinion about some obscure aspect of California tax law related to a case she was working on. After she'd heard what he'd had to say, she had thanked him, then proceeded to disagree with his interpretation of the law.

He got up and crossed over to the windows and looked out at the traffic going by. Most of the smog was gone now, and it looked as though it was going to be a hot, sunny day. He thought about Ellen and her wanting to get together with him. What was it Churchill said about Russia?...That it's a riddle wrapped in a mystery inside an enigma. Ditto Ellen, he thought.

He stepped out to tell Dottie that he was expecting news reporters around eleven o'clock or so who would no doubt want to question him about the kidnapping.

She gave him a sympathetic look. "You're getting more and more involved in this than you want to be, aren't you?"

"Sure looks that way," he said.

She pushed her glasses back against the bridge of her nose. "Norm wanted to see you before he left, but you were busy on the phone. He just wanted to see how you're feeling this morning, he said. And he said to tell you he's gone to Monterey Park on that auto injury case."

Michael thanked her and went back into his office. He got the Kenworthy file out of his attaché case, and started making critical last-minute changes on the brief. In what seemed a very short time, his phone rang and Dottie said, "The reporters are here, Michael."

He glanced at his watch. Ten-fifty. "I'll be right out," he said.

There must have been at least twenty reporters, cameramen, and photographers crowded into the outer office. And the moment he stepped out, there was pandemonium. Cameras whirred and clicked and flashed, and reporters started shouting questions at him.

"Hold on a second!" he shouted. "If you want any answers, you're going to have to quiet down and ask them one at a time."

The level of noise dropped a bit, and he spent the next fifteen minutes trying to answer their questions. A few of the reporters were brash, even insulting. But most of them were courteous and respectful, and he didn't mind trying to give them the information they wanted. He realized, however, that he didn't add very much to what they'd already learned from their session with the police department.

Chapter 7

After the last of the photographers, reporters and cameramen had gone, Dottie turned to him and said, "I'm proud of you, Michael. You handled them like a real pro."

"You mean I out shouted them?" he said, smiling.

"I mean you spoke right up and didn't let them intimidate you."

He laughed. "You're true-blue, Dottie." He glanced at his watch. "Well, like it or not, I guess I'd better get back to work. If I work right through the lunch hour, I should have the Kenworthy material all ready for you."

"You shouldn't be skipping lunches, Michael. It isn't good for you."

"I know," he said, shrugging.

"Should I bring you a sandwich or something when I come back from lunch?"

"No, thanks, Dottie. I'm really not at all hungry."

When Dottie came back close to an hour later, he had the Kenworthy material ready for her. He explained what he wanted done, then got right to work on a case involving the fraudulent sale of some valuable real estate by a local realtor.

Although he tried hard to concentrate, he couldn't help thinking of Carlene Edwards and how worried and upset her family must be. Finally he decided to stop what he was doing and try to contact Carlene's mother and see whether he could be of any help to her.

He remembered that the newscaster that morning had said her mother lived on Clayton Street, so he looked for the name Edwards in the phone book and found only one Edwards listed on that street, an H.M. Edwards.

When he dialed the number, a woman answered at once. "Helen Edwards speaking," she said in a businesslike voice. "May I help you?"

"I hope so," he said. "I'm Michael Donovan. I'm an attorney here in Pasadena. Are you Carlene Edwards' mother?"

"Why, yes, I am," the woman said after a slight pause. Her voice was a bit wary. "What is it you want?"

He didn't know quite what to say. "I don't know whether you know it, but Carlene ran into my office when she was trying to get away from the men who kidnapped her."

The woman didn't say anything.

"I'd like to help you in any way I can," he said. "I have some free time now, and I'd be glad to drop by for a few minutes and tell you what happened...that is, if it wouldn't inconvenience you."

She still didn't say anything.

He felt embarrassed. "I'm not doing this because I want you as a client. It' s just that..."

"All right," she said, her voice softening. "You're welcome to come out any time you like. It's nice of you to offer. I want to hear what happened to my daughter, of course."

"I'll see you in about twenty minutes, then," he said. "Goodbye, Mrs. Edwards."

He stepped out to tell Dottie what he was going to do.

"Why, that's very nice of you, Michael," she said. She nodded approvingly. "I'm sure she'll appreciate it."

"Look," he said. "There's no point in your staying around here any longer this afternoon. Why don't you lock up and take off?"

"I can't. I'm still working on the Kenworthy file."

"Oh, forget it. Do it tomorrow."

"It won't take much longer to finish it now. I might as well stay until it's all done."

He gave her a grateful smile. "I don't know what Norm and I would do without you, Dottie."

It didn't take long to reach Clayton Street. As he drove along the row of small, neat homes, he noticed a car coming toward him. He noticed it because it was moving so slowly, and the man and the woman in the front seat were peering at the homes on the south side of the street, just as he was. And then he realized, surprised, that the man and the woman in the car looked like the couple he'd seen yesterday in the hall outside his office, and later on, out by the parking garage. The man was thin and bald-headed, and the woman was short and plump and sandy-haired.

Michael frowned. What the devil were they doing out here?

As the car moved on by, he saw a man slouched in the backseat. The man was big and black-bearded.

My God, he thought, could it be the man who bashed him over the head and helped kidnap Carlene Edwards?...The man who made that sickening phone call to him?

Gripping the steering wheel, Michael made a quick U-turn at the next corner and sped back down the street, looking for the car. He wasn't sure, but he thought it was blue, and it looked like a Ford Tempo. If he could get its license plate number, he could have Lt. Ferraro check it out.

He drove several blocks down the street, but couldn't see the car anywhere. It must have turned down one of the side streets when he was making the U-turn.

He made another U-turn at the corner and. headed back down Clayton, feeling a bit foolish. Surely the black-bearded man he'd just seen couldn't be the black-bearded kidnapper. Why would anyone involved in a kidnapping risk driving by the home of the girl he'd just kidnapped?...The very place her sister's car had been firebombed? It didn't make sense.

It took only a few seconds to locate the Edwards' home. It was a small white stucco house, set well back from the street. It was neat and well-kept, with a patch of lawn and some shrubs in front. A wooden ramp went from the sidewalk up to the front porch. A carport was attached to the far side of the house.

He parked at the curb in front and walked on up the sidewalk. As he approached the wooden ramp, he noticed, off to his right, a big black scorched area on the concrete driveway. He supposed it was where Carlene's sister's car had been firebombed.

He rang the doorbell, and moments later, the door behind the screen door swung open. A thin African-American woman sat there in a wheelchair. She had a nice face and attractive white hair, and she was wearing a long-sleeved white blouse and black slacks.

"You must be Mr. Donovan," she said. "I'm Helen Edwards. Please come in."

He opened the screen door and stepped in. He could see then that her eyes were red and puffy, probably from lack of sleep and from crying.

"Sorry about your daughter and what happened here last night," he said awkwardly.

She nodded, her mouth tightening, and motioned with one hand toward a closed door on the other side of the hall.

"That part of the house serves as my office," she said. "I don't know whether you know it, but I run a telephone answering service here."

"No, I didn't know," he said.

She shrugged. "I guess you wouldn't unless you looked in the yellow pages. Anyhow, I'm lucky to have a daughter helping me operate the business for the next few days. She's in there now, so we can take all the time we need to." She started maneuvering the wheelchair down the hall toward a doorway to the right of them. "Follow me, please. We can talk in our living quarters over here."

The room they entered was furnished with maple furniture and beige drapes and cream-colored carpeting. It was neat and clean and comfortable looking.

She pointed to the armchair across from her. "Please take that chair, Mr. Donovan. I think you'll find it more comfortable than the others." She paused. "Is there anything you'd like to drink? Coffee? Tea?"

He shook his head. "No, thank you." He crossed over and sat down. He could see a photograph of Carlene on the mantel of the brick fireplace. Alongside it were photographs of two other attractive young women. Both of them resembled Carlene.

Mrs. Edwards positioned her wheelchair next to the coffee table so that she faced him.

"I have multiple sclerosis," she said in a calm, matter-of-fact voice, "and I've been in this wheelchair off and on for almost ten years. I can still get out of it, though, if I have to. I don't tell you this to get your sympathy. I tell you so you won't have to waste time wondering what's wrong with me or feeling sorry for me. I get along quite well, and I make sure to tell that to everybody I meet for the first time. So now that I've got that done, please tell me about Carlene and what happened yesterday."

As gently as he could, Michael told her about the kidnapping. When he finished, she looked down at her hands, which were clenched together on her lap. For a few moments, she didn't say anything. Then she looked up, and he could tell that she was trying hard to keep from crying.

"I wanted to tell all the reporters who were here today just what I thought of the wicked people who did this to my girls," she said, her voice trembling. "But I didn't. I didn't want to say or do anything that might anger the people holding Carlene that might set them off, so to speak. I didn't want them to take it out on her, and I didn't want them trying to hurt my other girls. I didn't, and I don't, want to do anything that might make them harm them."

Michael felt a twinge of guilt. She'd been a lot smarter than he had. He'd told the reporters he thought the kidnappers were dirty bastards, or words to that effect.

"I've talked to Lieutenant Ferraro of the Pasadena Police Department," he said, "and you probably have, too. I know the police are working very hard on this. And I understand the FBI is working with them. So they're bound to come up with something. And soon. They're bound to find Carlene, and get her safely back to you."

The lines around Mrs. Edwards' mouth deepened. "I pray to God you're right," she said. "Even though I'm a Christian woman, I don't think I can forgive the people who did this terrible thing. Carlene never did a single thing in her whole life to hurt anybody. In all her eighteen years of living, I don't think she's ever made an enemy. She's a decent girl, a moral girl, and she..." She paused and looked toward the doorway.

An obviously pregnant young African-American woman, probably in her mid-twenties, stood there. She was quite pretty and looked a lot like Carlene, and she was wearing a light blue maternity smock.

"Excuse me for interrupting," she said to Mrs. Edwards. "But Margaret is on the phone. Do you want to talk to her? Or should I tell her you'll call her back? She says she's driving out to Arcadia in an hour or so."

"Tell her I'll call her back before she leaves," Mrs. Edwards said. She turned to Michael. "This is my daughter Belinda."

"I'm glad to meet you," Michael said, standing up.

"I'm glad to meet you, too," her daughter said. "We're very grateful to you for trying to help Carlene."

Mrs. Edwards smiled at her daughter. "Belinda is expecting her first baby in late February. It will be my first grandchild."

Her daughter gave her mother an embarrassed but affectionate smile.

"If you'll excuse me," she said, "I'll get back to work. I'll tell Margaret you'll call her a little later." She looked at Michael.

"Nice to meet you, Mr. Donovan."

"Thank you, Belinda. Nice to meet you."

After the girl left, Michael turned, still standing, to Mrs. Edwards.

"I'd better go now," he said. He paused. "Is there anything I can do for you...anything I can do to help?"

Mrs. Edwards shook her head. "You're very kind, but no, there isn't. What I can't do for myself, Belinda and her husband do for me. And my other daughter when she's in town is glad to help too."

"Well, if you should think of anything, don't hesitate to call me." He took out his billfold and gave her one of his business cards. "I'll be glad to help in any way I can."

"Thank you, Mr. Donovan." Her eyes reddened with emotion. "I do appreciate your kindness."

Chapter 8

He pulled into the parking lot in back of Charlie's, glad to be driving his little red Cavalier again. He looked for Ellen's Porsche, but didn't see it. Not that he expected to. Ellen had many virtues, but punctuality wasn't one of them.

He parked as close to the backdoor as he could, not wanting a repeat of last night's paint job on his car, and went on in. He sat at the bar and ordered a vodka gimlet on the rocks.

Dave, the bartender, asked whether he'd heard anything new about the kidnapping. Michael shook his head. "Not a thing."

"That was a rotten thing that happened out at the girl's home last night, wasn't it?...Firebombing her sister's car that way."

"It sure was," said Michael.

A big, heavyset man came in and sat down at the end of the bar.

"Excuse me," Dave said, and went down to take the man's order.

Michael took a sip of his drink, hoping the pain he'd felt in his stomach the last day or two wasn't signaling the return of his ulcer.

Dave came back and started to discuss the upcoming Rose Bowl game, but had to stop to fill an order for one of the waitresses.

Michael finished his drink, and as he put down his glass, he saw Ellen in the big mirror behind the bar. She was coming toward him, looking trim and attractive in a dark-gray suit. He got off the stool to greet her, his pulse quickening.

"Sorry I'm late," she said, stepping up to him with a warm smile and kissing his cheek. "How are you, Mike?"

"I'm fine," he said. "How're you, Ellen?"

"Couldn't be better, thanks. How's your head?" She looked at the bump above his ear.

"It's all right. It wasn't much to begin with."

"That isn't what Ruth said when I talked to her this morning."

"Believe me, it's all right." He took her elbow, aware of the pleasant, familiar scent of her perfume. "Let's find a booth so we can have some privacy."

They walked down the stairs into the main room and on down toward the fireplace. Jan Ashby wasn't at the piano, but he supposed she would be coming in any time now.

He indicated a booth off to the left of them. "This okay?"

"Fine," she smiled.

She slipped behind the table with a silky rustling sound and settled back against the leather upholstery. He sat down across from her, thinking how pretty she looked with her dark hair brushed back from her forehead that way.

Jeannie, the waitress, a part-time student at Cal State, came up to the booth.

"Take your order, Mr. Donovan?"

"Yes, Jeannie." He turned to Ellen. "What'll you have? Your usual?"

"Please."

He gave Jeannie their order and when she left, Ellen reached over and put her hand on his.

"I've been dying all day to hear what happened yesterday, Mike. It must've been very upsetting."

Although he didn't want to talk about it, he gave her a brief account of what happened. When he finished, her eyes glinted with anger.

"What a terrible experience! For both of you. I remember seeing pictures of that poor girl in the paper. She looked so young and innocent. And she couldn't be prettier."

Jeannie returned with their drinks, then left, and Ellen said, "The kidnappers haven't tried to get in touch with anybody, have they?"

He picked up his drink, rotating the ice cubes. "As a matter of fact one of them called me last night."

"You're kidding!"

"No, I'm serious."

"What did he want? What did he say?"

"It was disgusting. He said a lot of rotten things about the minorities in our country. And then he made some kind of veiled threat about what he and his cohorts were going to do next. And then, no more than an hour or two after his phone call, those bastards went out and firebombed the girl's sister's car."

"It's frightening, isn't it?"

"Yes, it is. And it's not just an isolated incident. There have been other kidnappings and firebombings and shootings in other places in the country. I understand that some of these white supremacists and militias are in constant touch with one another through computer networks. And I understand they are storing up huge amounts of arms and bomb-making materials and are targeting federal buildings all across the country."

Her eyes hardened. "They're completely mad!"

"I agree. They're crazy."

She leaned forward and put her hand on his. "I can guess how much you're emotionally involved in this because of the girl. I know how you are about such things. You're just a big softy, Mike."

He tried to smile. "Oh, I don't know about that, Ellen. I think I'm pretty tough."

"Tough, Mike?" She frowned and withdrew her hand. "The truth is, you're just like your dad. You're too good-hearted for your own sake. You could be making ten times what you're making now if you'd just put that keen legal mind of yours where the money is and let others handle the pro bono cases, the charity cases."

"I like what I'm doing, Ellen."

"But why not let others do it, people like Norm? I've told you a thousand times there are several first-rate firms here in Pasadena that would love to have you."

"Ellen, you're a sweet gal, and I appreciate your confidence in me. But I'd really rather talk about something else. Let's talk about you, for instance, and what's new or different in your life."

"I don't want to bore you, Mike."

"I'd really like to know, Ellen."

"Well, I'm afraid you're going to have to wait awhile." She was looking at someone or something over his shoulder.

Michael turned and saw Jan Ashby coming toward them. She was wearing a pale-blue dress that accentuated her slim blondeness, and she looked bright-eyed and excited.

"Hi, Ellen," she cried. Then she turned to Michael. "I just saw you on TV," she exclaimed. "On the news. Why didn't you say something about it last night? About the kidnapping, I mean." Her tone was reproving.

Michael shrugged. "There wasn't much to say." He smiled at her. "Anyhow, I'm the silent type, y'know."

She smiled back at him. "Now I know why you had that bump on your head." She bent and peered at the bump above his ear. "Looks much better now, doesn't it?" She straightened up. "By the way, I thought you handled that mob of reporters magnificently. I've never heard such rude and impertinent questions in all my life. You'd think they thought it was you who kidnapped the girl."

"I suppose it's just their way of getting a story," he said. He hesitated. "Care to join us for a drink, Jan?" He started to move over so she could sit down beside him.

She put her hand on his shoulder, stopping him. "Wish I could. But I'm a few minutes late as is. Is there anything either of you would like to hear?" She smiled at Ellen. "Mike likes anything by Cole Porter or George Gershwin, you know."

Ellen's smile looked a bit forced. "Yes, I know." She turned to Michael. "Why don't you decide, Mike?"

Jan looked at Michael. "Well, Mike, what's it to be?"

"Oh, I'll leave that up to you, Jan."

She flashed him a warm smile. "I'll try not to disappoint you," she said. She turned to go. "Enjoy yourselves," she said over her shoulder.

Michael looked across at Ellen with a wry smile. "Now, Ellen, getting back to what we were talking about, tell me what you've been doing the last few months. Interesting cases you've had...people you've met...things you've done."

She took a sip of her drink. "Sad to say, I haven't had any interesting cases recently. But I have learned a great deal researching all kinds of legal esoterica in the law library. In fact, I've spent so much time there I thought I'd surely run into you." She paused and looked toward Jan Ashby, who had begun playing a bright, jazzy version of Cole Porter's "Anything Goes."

They listened without talking until Jan was through. Then Jan looked their way and began to play and sing another Cole Porter favorite of Michael's, "Easy to Love." Her soft, clear voice gave the lyrics a special kind of intimacy that seemed to radiate all the way across the room to them.

When Jan finished, neither of them said anything for a few moments, then Ellen said, "Jan's in love with you, Mike. You know that, don't you?"

"We're just friends, Ellen."

She gave him an apologetic little shrug. "I know it's none of my business, but even Ruth's mentioned it."

"It's all very innocent, Ellen. I never see her except when I'm here."

"I'm sure she'd jump at the chance to go out with you."

"I doubt it. She's friendly with all the guys."

"Oh, Mike. You can be so naive about some things."

He smiled. "So I'm naive."

"About women, yes."

"Well, maybe so. But enough about me. Tell me, Ellen, who's the big love interest in your life now?"

"What do you mean 'now'? You make it sound as though there's been a long succession of them."

"All right. I'll rephrase that. Are you dating anyone in particular now?"

She hesitated. "Yes, I am."

He tried to sound casual. "Anyone I know?"

"I don't think so."

"Is it serious?"

"I'm not sure. It's too soon to tell." She stirred her drink with the swizzle stick. "He's an orthopedic surgeon. Ronald Putnam. You may have heard of him. He has his practice here in Pasadena."

"Oh," he said, surprised. "I think maybe I do know him. But only slightly. He testified in a case I had a small part in last summer." He felt a pang of jealousy. He didn't want her interested in anyone else, going out with anyone else. "How did you meet him?" His lips felt stiff, dry.

"At a party our firm had. We handled a lawsuit for him a couple of months ago."

"I presume he's not married."

"Of course not." Her eyes glinted with indignation. "You know me better than that, Mike."

His eyes softened. "Yes, of course, I do, Ellen." He made little circles on the table with his glass. "Has he ever been married?"

"Yes. Once. He's divorced now. Has two children. Both girls. One nine. The other six. His ex-wife has them."

He took a long drink, put the glass down, empty. He could feel his stomach start to knot up, to burn. This Putnam was smart and quite good-looking, quite sophisticated. He didn't like the thought of her falling in love with him.

She glanced at her watch, then looked across at him with a wry smile.

"Sorry, Mike, but I'm going to have to run along now. I'm already late for another appointment."

"With Putnam?"

"Yes." She picked up her purse from the seat beside her. "We have a dinner date."

"I'll walk you to your car," he said.

He got up and she slipped out from behind the table and stood up beside him. He thought of her long, smooth legs and her small waist and her lovely, lithe body, and the thought of Putnam or anybody else making love to her made him feel sick inside.

He took her arm and they turned and started toward the stairs. He didn't look back at Jan Ashby to wave goodbye.

When they got outside, he was relieved to see that his car looked unharmed. They went on down the row of cars to her white Porsche. She got her car key out of her purse, and he took it from her and unlocked and opened the door for her. She smiled and he kissed her lightly on the cheek, fighting the impulse to pull her to him and kiss her on the lips, hard.

"Thanks for the drink, Mike," she said. "And do let me hear from you, won't you?"

"I will, Ellen. Keep your doors locked and drive carefully."

She slipped behind the steering wheel, and he closed the door for her and waited while she started the engine and backed out. She smiled and waved to him through the window as she headed toward the exit.

He turned and walked back toward his car, suddenly feeling tired and depressed. The thought of going to his apartment and spending the rest of the night working on the files in his attaché case was repugnant.

Chapter 9

The first thing he did when he got to his apartment was look at the *Times*. The banner headline seemed to leap off the front page—PASADENA ROSE QUEEN KIDNAPPED. Just below was a photograph of Carlene, looking young and innocent and winsome.

He glanced at the accompanying stories of the kidnapping and the firebombing of Carlene's sister's car. He didn't learn anything he hadn't already known. There wasn't any mention of his name, of course. That would come in tomorrow's edition, no doubt.

It was all very depressing. He sighed and decided he'd better eat something, since he'd skipped lunch. He stuck a Swanson turkey dinner in the oven, then sat down to look at the rest of the paper and go through his mail.

After he'd eaten, he went into the den and worked on the files he'd brought home. He stopped at eleven o'clock and turned on the TV to see whether his encounter with the news media would be on the late news. And it was. Two minutes into the CNN newscast, he suddenly appeared on the screen, looking self-conscious and defiant. He was embarrassed by what he saw—his obvious discomfort, his pomposity. He was on the screen only a few seconds, then the newscast turned to another story.

He got up, chagrined, and turned off the TV. As he started back to his desk, the phone rang, startling him. He hesitated, hoping fervently it wouldn't be the black-bearded kidnapper.

He picked up the receiver. "Michael Donovan speaking," he said.

"Hello, Mr. Donovan," a woman's voice said. "Sorry to be calling this late, but I've got some information for you that won't wait, something you'd better listen to carefully." Her voice was husky, almost masculine.

His heart started thudding against his chest. "Who is this?" he asked.

"It isn't important that you know who I am, Mr. Donovan. But it is important that you hear what I've got to say. A friend of mine called you last night, and told you that you shouldn't have tried to protect that black girl. And that's why I'm calling. Now that you've got yourself involved in all this, we think it's only fair to let you know that we're planning even bigger and better things for those black friends of yours."

"Look," he said, gripping the receiver. "What are you trying to do? Why are you telling me all this?"

"Don't worry," the woman said. "You'll find out soon enough. But before we get into that, I'd better tell you it will be useless to try to trace this call. If you're smart, you'll concentrate on what I have to say. First, we want you to know you're not helping that girl one whit by allying yourself with her family. In fact, you're only making matters worse for her. Second, we saw you meeting with members of the news media this morning on TV, and we were very disturbed by what you said about us. Those were mean and spiteful words, Mr. Donovan...especially coming from a white man. You're just asking for trouble when you say things like that. It forces us to do things to the girl that—"

"I'm warning you," he broke in. He almost choked on the words. "You'd better not harm her, and you'd better let her go. Right now. The FBI is involved in—"

"It isn't going to do any good threatening us," the woman said, raising her voice above his.

"You're crazy!" he cried. "You're all crazy! Why are you doing this to the girl? She's not harming you...or anybody else. And why are you calling me? Why are you telling me all this rot?"

"Because you're the enemy, Mr. Donovan. All you bleeding heart do-gooders and pinko liberals and ACLUers."

"But what does that have to do with the girl? I told you, she hasn't harmed anybody. Let her go for God's sake! She's—"

"I was just coming to that," the woman interrupted, her voice hard and scathing. "If you think kidnapping that little black animal and blowing up her sister's car was bad, just wait till you find out what we've got planned next."

"I warn you. You'd better stop all this madness or—"

"Or what, Mr. Lawyer? Your threats and bluster don't scare me one tiny bit." She paused. "But I'm not going to say any more now. All you bleeding hearts will just have to wait to find out what's going to happen next. But I can tell you this much. You're going to be in for another big surprise. One that will make you know we mean business for sure, that we aren't wasting any more time just fooling around. You'll see."

Before he could say anything, she banged down the receiver, cutting him off.

He stood there for a few seconds, his stomach cramping, his heart racing. Then he dropped the receiver back in place. It was too late to call Lt. Ferraro at his home. Maybe he'd better call the police department instead. He looked up the number in the phone book, dialed it, and someone answered at once.

"Pasadena Police Department," a man said. "Sergeant Frost speaking."

"This is Michael Donovan," Michael said. "I'm an attorney here in Pasadena. I was with the Rose Queen, Carlene Edwards, when she was kidnapped, and I just received a threatening phone call here at home from some woman who's evidently involved in the kidnapping. She informed me that they're going to do something worse than what they did to the Rose Queen's sister's car. I know it sounds crazy, but she's serious. So I thought I'd better let you know. If you want to, you can check my name and number in the phone book and call me back to verify this. Or you can call Lieutenant Ferraro at his home, and he'll vouch for me. He questioned me right after the kidnapping and told me to keep in touch with him, but I hated to disturb him this late at night."

"Don't worry, Mr. Donovan," the sergeant said. "You don't know me, but I happen to know you through some of your court appearances. I'll inform my superior officer, and I'm sure he'll take action on this right away."

"Good. Please don't think I'm trying to tell you or your fellow officers what to do, but I think it would be wise to post someone outside the kidnapped girl's home for the rest of the night or for as long as you think it might be necessary."

"We're doing that right now, Mr. Donovan. We've been keeping surveillance on the Edwards' home since yesterday, particularly since the firebombing."

"Well," said Michael, relieved, "I'm glad to hear that."

"But just to be doubly sure." the sergeant said, "I'll see that the officers patrolling that area are informed right away about the threat. And I'll also ask my superior officer to inform all other personnel on duty and caution them to be on the lookout for trouble."

"The kidnapped girl's mother is an invalid," Michael said, "and the daughter staying with her is pregnant. They're all alone there, and really vulnerable."

"Don't worry, Mr. Donovan. We'll take care of it right away. In fact, I'll get right to it. Thanks very much for alerting us."

When Michael hung up, his fingers were stiff from gripping the receiver, and his stomach felt as though it was on fire.

He sighed and tried to relax. It would be impossible to do any more work now. He wouldn't be able to concentrate. The work he was doing was complex and technical and required a great deal of thought.

He went to the bathroom, washed his hands and face, and brushed his teeth, and then went into the bedroom. The orangish glow of the electric clock on the bedside table showed 11.40. He got into bed and lay there for what seemed a long time before he fell asleep.

When he awoke, he was surprised to see Ellen coming toward him. She was dressed in a clinging white nylon nightgown that he'd always liked and she looked slim and lovely and she was smiling and looked glad to see him. He got up and she came up to him and slipped her arms around his neck and he felt his chest tighten and suddenly all his old love for her came rushing back.

"Oh. Mike," she sighed, "I'm so glad to see you! I do love you, darling. You know that, don't you? I'll never love anyone else. That silly doctor means nothing to me. Absolutely nothing."

She raised her face to kiss him and suddenly it wasn't her face but the dark frightened face of the kidnapped girl. Carlene Edwards.

"Please help me, Mr. Donovan," the girl was sobbing. "Please help me. I think they're going to kill me."

He sat up, his heart pounding. It took several seconds for him to realize where he was and that he'd been dreaming.

He glanced at the clock. Ten after six. The alarm would go off in five more minutes. He reached over turned off the alarm, and got up.

By the time he'd showered and shaved and had some orange juice, toast, and coffee, it was almost seven o'clock. He poured himself another cup of coffee and turned on the radio to get the news.

He was almost afraid to listen. Who knew what that crazy woman and those degenerates might have been up to since she called last night?

After the station break and the usual commercials, the seven o'clock news came on.

"There has been another development in the kidnapping of the Tournament of Roses Queen," the newscaster said. "Shortly after eleven o'clock last night, the Pasadena home of Helen Edwards, the kidnapped Rose Queen's widowed mother, was firebombed and gutted. Firemen responding to the fire were unable to rescue the only two occupants of the one-story house, the Rose Queen's invalid mother and her older married sister. Tragically, both of them perished in the fire. According to a close friend of Mrs. Edwards, the married sister was pregnant with her first child..."

Michael's stomach cramped. He reached out and turned off the radio, his eyes blurring. *My God, while that lousy bitch was talking to him on the phone last night, those degenerate accomplices of hers were firebombing the Edwards' home. And that lousy bitch knew it. It was a cold-blooded, premeditated act, and she was a knowing participant.*

He gagged and went to the bathroom and vomited what little breakfast he'd eaten into the toilet.

Chapter 10

At ten-thirty that same morning, Dottie ushered FBI Agent Carlton Bryce into Michael's office. Agent Bryce looked trim and fit in a dark-blue suit, white shirt, and dark-red tie.

"I want to thank you for seeing me on such short notice," he said, shaking Michael's hand. "I meant to get to you sooner, but I just wasn't able to. I'm sure you know our office is cooperating with the Pasadena police on this case."

"That's what I understand," Michael said. "Please sit down." He indicated the chair across from him.

Agent Bryce thanked him and sat down. "Lieutenant Ferraro has given me a complete rundown on your part in all this," he said, "so I won't ask you to repeat any of the details...that is, unless you feel there's something you'd like to emphasize or there's something you've thought of since you last talked to Lieutenant Ferraro."

Michael shook his head. "No, I don't believe there is."

Agent Bryce's eyes hardened. "I suppose you heard about the firebombing of the Edwards' home last night, didn't you?"

Michael nodded. "It's tragic. I went out to visit Mrs. Edwards yesterday afternoon, and while I was there, she introduced me to the daughter who was there helping her, the pregnant one. I never dreamt anything like this would happen to them."

"Mind if I ask why you visited Mrs. Edwards?"

"Why, no. Of course not. I'm sure Lieutenant Ferraro told you I was with her daughter, who's the Rose Queen, when she was kidnapped. Anyway, I thought I should tell Mrs. Edwards what I knew about the kidnapping and see if there was anything I could do to help her."

"I see."

"There's something else I think I should mention," Michael said. "I don't know how important it is or whether it will help, but when I drove out to see Mrs. Edwards I thought I saw one of the two men who kidnapped the girl, the one who bashed my head with his gun. He was in a car with a man and a woman, and they were driving by Mrs. Edwards' home, and they seemed to be looking it over. Anyway, I'm quite sure the man and the woman with him were the ones I'd seen the same day the girl was kidnapped. The first time I saw them was in the hallway down from my office, after the girl came bursting through my door, and the second time was later that same day outside our parking garage, after the girl had been kidnapped."

"Lieutenant Ferraro said you tried to get the license number of their car but couldn't."

Michael grimaced. "That's right. They must've driven down some side street while I was turning around. Anyway, they got away."

"Do you know what kind of car they were driving?"

"I think it was a Ford Tempo, a four-door sedan. And it was a fairly late model, and it was blue."

"You didn't say who was driving it."

"It was the man with the woman. They were in the front seat, and the man who bashed me on the head, the kidnapper, was in the backseat. I didn't get too good a look at them, but the man was thin and bald-headed, and the woman was short and plump and had sandy colored hair. That's not a very good description, I know. But I'd definitely recognize them if I saw them again."

"Lieutenant Ferraro said you told him the man who helped kidnap the girl has a black beard and is three or four inches over six feet. Is that so?"

"Yes. He's very big and heavy-set, and his beard is carefully trimmed, that is, cut short."

"And the other man who helped kidnap the girl has red hair, and quite a lot of it, you said."

"Yes, that's right. Please understand, though, I didn't get a really good look at either one of them. They came up behind the girl and me and caught us by surprise."

"That's what I understand," Agent Bryce said, nodding.

Michael paused. "I guess I should mention that the black-bearded man called me at home the other night...that is, the night before last, to be precise. And he made all kinds of threatening and degrading racist remarks."

"Lieutenant Ferraro told me about that, too," Agent Bryce said.

"I also received a call last night from a woman who indicated that she was involved with the kidnapping," Michael said. "She evidently called about the same time the Edwards' home was being firebombed. She warned me that they were planning some kind of surprise that would show how serious they were about changing the way this country is run."

"Yes, I know. This White Unity organization they belong to is just one of several radical organizations we're keeping under surveillance all across the nation. Some of the militias and Ku Klux Klan groups have links with them, and also some of the neo-Nazi groups, which are extremely radical. In fact, one of these groups has the weird idea that Christ was an Aryan and that white Anglo-Saxons are the chosen people of God, not the Jews. They believe that the lost tribes of Israel were Anglo-Saxons and other Aryan races and that the United States is the Promised Land of the Bible and that Jews are the children of Satan. And they believe that the blacks are the children of Satan, too, of course."

"It's crazy, unbelievable!"

"I know. But, no matter how crazy their beliefs are, we mustn't underestimate any of these organizations. They're very clever and very dangerous. They have lists of people and groups they regard as their mortal enemies. And they're preparing to attack them whenever and wherever they can. The ACLU is high' on all these lists. I understand that you and your partner are quite active in the ACLU. Is that so?"

"Yes, we both are."

"That probably explains why they've targeted you for special attention. "

Michael shrugged and, leaning forward, clasped his hands together on his desk.

"Has Lieutenant Ferraro learned anything more about the kidnappers...or developed any leads?" he asked.

Agent Bryce shook his head. "No, I'm afraid not. To my knowledge, you're the only one they've contacted directly."

"And what about you? Have you or any of your agents learned anything new?"

"No, only what we've learned through Lieutenant Ferraro and his department."

"Is that a good omen or bad?"

"Hard to say. It's been only a couple of days now since the kidnapping. Judging from my experience in these matters, that's a relatively short time. They may try to get in touch with you again and soon...or they might get in touch with some public official or prominent member of the news media" He shrugged. "But who knows? Who knows what they're up to? I don't want to sound pessimistic or morbid, and I hate to say it, but it's possible that we may never hear from the kidnappers again. Or from the girl."

The thought chilled Michael.

"It happens in quite a number of cases. The kidnappers are never apprehended and the victim is found dead somewhere or is never found." He glanced at his watch and got to his feet. "Well, Mr. Donovan, I've taken up more of your time than I should've. But I did want to check in with you and get your reaction to all this."

Michael stood up, too. "I'm glad you did."

Agent Bryce reached for his billfold. "I'll be working closely with Lieutenant Ferraro and his department on this, but I'd like to give you my card, which has both my office and home phone numbers on it." He drew a card out of his billfold and handed it to Michael. "In case anything comes up and you can't get in touch with Lieutenant Ferraro, don't hesitate to call me at either of these numbers."

"I'll be sure to do that," Michael said. He slipped the card into his billfold next to Lt. Ferraro's.

Agent Bryce held out his hand. "Thanks for your time and cooperation, Mr. Donovan."

"You're welcome," Michael said, shaking hands with him and walking him to the outer door.

After Agent Bryce left, Michael walked back into his office and looked down through the windows at the traffic below. Still no word on Carlene Edwards…except for the crazy phone calls he'd received. Was it possible they had already killed her…or were going to?

Suddenly he wanted very much to talk to Ellen, to hear her reassuring, no-nonsense voice.

He went to his desk picked up the receiver and dialed her number. He was in luck. Her secretary informed him that Ellen would be with him in just a moment.

He had just settled back in his chair when her voice came through the receiver, warm and cheerful.

"My," she exclaimed, "what a pleasant surprise! You caught me just in time. I was just getting ready to leave for the law library."

"Did you hear about the firebombing last night?"

"Firebombing? I don't know what you're talking about, Mike. I've been in conference all morning. You don't mean what they did to that girl's car, do you?"

"No, that's not it. The Edwards' home was firebombed last night."

"The kidnapped girl's home?"

"Yes. Her mother and her older sister were there. They were burned to death."

"Oh, no!" she gasped.

"Her sister was pregnant...expecting her first baby in a couple of months. Or did I tell you that last night?"

"Yes, you did. I...I feel just sick about this, Mike. How could anyone be so cruel?"

"They're degenerates, Ellen."

"Have they caught who did it?"

"No. No such luck."

Ellen, who was always quick to control her emotions, spoke in a calmer voice now.

"You must feel terrible about this, Mike."

"That's why I'm calling, Ellen. I need some cheering up. Could I buy you a drink after work tonight?"

"Oh, I'm sorry. I'd love to see you. But I can't. I have another engagement."

"With the orthopedist?"

"Yes."

He tried to sound nonchalant. "Well, I'm sorry we can't get together."

"So am I, Mike. Why don't you call me sometime next week?"

"I'll do that."

"Sorry about this evening."

"That's all right, Ellen, I understand. Have a good time."

He said goodbye and hung up, hoping passionately that she wouldn't have a good time—hoping, in fact, that she'd have a lousy time. What did she see in that supercilious orthopedist, anyhow?

Chapter 11

Early that afternoon, Michael headed out for St. Luke's Hospital to take a statement from a friend of his and Ellen's who had been injured in a car accident.

He hadn't driven very far when he noticed, not far behind him, a familiar-looking blue Ford Tempo with two men in the front seat. It looked as though the one driving was bald-headed, and the other one, black-bearded.

He stiffened in surprise. Good God! It couldn't be!

At the first intersection he came to, he abruptly turned north to see whether the car would try to follow him. He was relieved when it didn't. In his rearview mirror, he saw it continue on through the intersection, going east.

He relaxed. Evidently it wasn't who he'd thought it was. When he reached the hospital, Bill Gray, a freelance court reporter friend of his, was waiting for him in the lobby.

"Hi, Bill," Michael said. "Afraid there's been a slight change of plans. The attorney representing the girl who ran into Mrs. Ward had to cancel the deposition. His secretary called just before I left my office to tell me that he'd suddenly become ill. She said he'd get in touch with me later this week to reschedule the deposition. I called to let you know, but you'd already left your office. So I decided to go ahead and take a statement from Mrs. Ward and, if necessary, do the deposition later on. Hope you don't mind."

"Not at all, Mike. Glad to help any way I can."

Michael shifted his attaché case to his other hand. "Before we go up to see Mrs. Ward, I'd better tell you something I didn't mention on the phone. I think I told you she fractured a couple of ribs and one of her ankles in the accident, and that the seventeen-year-old girl who ran into her was charged with driving under the influence of alcohol. But what I didn't tell you is that when the doctors X-rayed Mrs. Ward's chest, they discovered that her lungs were full of cancer. They've given her less than six months to live."

"Why, that's terrible."

Michael nodded. "It really is. She's only thirty-eight."

"Does she know about the prognosis?"

"Oh, yes. She was devastated at first. But you'd never know it now. You'd think her only concern was to get home to her two daughters and back to her students. I told you she's an elementary school teacher, didn't I?"

"Yes, you did. And you said she's a single parent."

"And has been for about five years, since her husband died in a plane crash. He was a pilot with the Air Force."

"A sad situation, isn't it?"

"Yes, it is. I thought you'd better know what she's facing before we go up there." He checked his watch. "We're due there in just a couple of minutes, so I guess we'd better get going."

Mrs. Ward was propped up against a couple of pillows when they walked into her room. Except for her salt-and-pepper hair, she looked much younger than thirty-eight. And, despite her illness, she looked bright-eyed and cheerful.

"Hello, Michael," she said, smiling. "I know it must be two-thirty or you wouldn't be here. No one's more dependable and punctual than you."

He returned her smile. "It's that obsessive-compulsive personality of mine, Martha. Did you get my message about having to cancel the deposition and do a statement instead?"

"Yes, I did."

"Sorry about that. We'll try to do the deposition later this week." He nodded at Bill Gray. "This is my friend Bill Gray. He's a court reporter and he'll record your statement."

"It's nice to meet you," she said.

"Thank you," said Bill. "Nice to meet you."

She turned to Michael. "Before we get started, I want to thank you for the lovely gladioluses. Their colors are just beautiful. They cheer me up every time I look at them."

"Glad you like them, Martha."

She smiled at Bill Gray. "If all lawyers were as nice as Michael, this would be a much nicer world."

Michael laughed . "What is this, anyway?...'Flatter-Your-Lawyer Day?" He put his hand on Bill's shoulder. "Well, Bill, if you're ready, I think we'd better get started." He turned to Mrs. Ward. "I'm simply going to ask you a series of questions, Martha, regarding the particulars of the accident. In effect, it's your statement or account of what happened. Mr. Gray will use that little stenographic machine he's carrying to record the date, time, and place of this statement, and he'll record all my questions and comments and your answers and anything else you might want to say. Now, are you ready?"

"Yes, Michael," she said, "I'm ready."

For the next fifteen minutes, Michael questioned her about the accident—when and where it occurred, who witnessed it, whether she had a valid driver's license and the state-required insurance coverage as well, who the officers were who were called to the scene of the accident, and so on.

"Well," he said finally, "I think that covers everything, Martha. Is there anything else you want to say?"

She shook her head. "No, I don't believe so, Michael. I believe that's about everything."

"Good enough. After Mr. Gray transcribes this, I'll get copies to you for your approval and signature."

Her eyes began to look a bit tearful. "I feel awfully sorry that the girl has to face that drunk-driving charge, Michael. She's so young...not much older than my girls, you know."

"I know," he said. And the truth was he felt sorry for the girl, too. But his heart ached for Martha.

After Michael and Bill said goodbye to her, they went down to the lobby together, then on out to the parking lot.

"Thanks, Bill, for your help on this," Michael said as they paused there a moment, blinking in the bright sunlight.

"You're welcome, Mike," Bill said. "I'll see that my secretary gets to work on it as soon as possible. And I'll get the copies to you as soon as they're done."

Michael's car was hot and stuffy when he slipped behind the steering wheel. He rolled down both front windows, turned the air conditioner on high, and headed out of the parking lot.

As he turned onto Washington Boulevard he glanced in his rearview mirror to check the traffic behind him. He saw a blue Ford Tempo swing into the lane directly behind him. A bald-headed man was driving and a big black-bearded man was seated next to him.

"Damn!" Michael exclaimed. There was no doubt about it this time. It was two of the thugs involved in the kidnapping. Evidently they had followed him to the hospital and then waited for him to come out.

But what the devil were they up to? Why the devil were they following him?

Chapter 12

Michael continued west on Washington Boulevard, with the blue Ford Tempo still close behind him.

What the devil should he do?...What could he do?...Should he head for police headquarters?...Look for a police car?

At the next corner, he made a sudden, sharp turn south, cutting dangerously close to a car coming toward him, hoping to lose them that way.

As he sped down Allen Avenue he checked his rearview mirror. He couldn't believe it! The blue Ford Tempo was still behind him. And bearing down fast. Suddenly it rammed into him, into his rear bumper, jolting him up against his seat belt. Before he could think straight, it rammed into him again. My God! What were they trying to do?

He slammed on his brakes, jerked off his seat belt, leapt out of the car. The blue Ford Tempo was rammed up against his rear bumper, and the bald-headed driver sat staring at him, his mouth agape, his eyes wide and startled looking. The black-bearded thug sat next to him, hunched against the dashboard, gasping for air.

Before the bald-headed thug could move, Michael jerked open the door and grabbed the front of his shirt.

"What the hell do you think you're doing?" he yelled.

The thug's face reddened. "You crazy?" he sputtered. "Let go of me, for chrissake!"

Michael tried to jerk him out of the car but couldn't. The thug's seatbelt was holding him back.

A couple of cars had stopped behind them, their horns blaring. The black-bearded thug leapt out of his side of the car and came rushing around the back end. Michael let go of the bald-headed thug and turned to face the black-bearded thug.

"You goddamn nigger lover!" the thug yelled, and swung his fist at Michael. Michael ducked and the thug's fist slammed into the open door behind Michael. Before Michael could straighten up, the thug lowered one shoulder and smashed into him. Michael twisted to one side and lashed out with his elbow. He caught the thug on his Adam's apple, and the thug choked and fell back against the car.

Suddenly someone slammed into Michael, knocking him off balance.

"Take it easy!" someone shouted, grabbing him around the neck.

Michael gasped and tried to twist free. Two men had pinned his arms to his sides and were forcing him around the back of the thugs' car toward the curb. Michael could see better now. The men were big and husky and wore work clothes. They forced him up against a tree next to the street.

"Let me go!" Michael yelled. "Stop them! They're kidnappers...murderers! They're getting away!"

He watched helplessly as the two thugs backed their car away from his, and with tires screeching, careened on down Allen Avenue.

"They kidnapped the Rose Queen!" Michael cried to the two men holding him. He could see now by the lettering on their work shirts that they were gardeners.

"They what?" one of the men said.

"They kidnapped the Rose Queen...burned down her house...killed her mother and sister!...They're murderers!"

The two men, looking sheepish, released him.

As Michael drove back to his office, he tried to figure out why the two thugs had followed him, had rammed into him. What the devil were they trying to do, anyhow?...Intimidate him?

But why would they want to do that? It didn't make sense...What would they accomplish? That woman who had called had said he was the enemy. But that was ridiculous. He certainly wasn't a threat to them. How could he be?

So what were they up to? He wasn't a black or a Hispanic or an Asian. That was obvious. And he wasn't a Jew, either. So what could it be? Was this their crazy, twisted way of getting revenge because he'd befriended Carlene Edwards and her family?...Because he'd publicly condemned the White Unity movement on TV?...Because he was active in the ACLU and promoted several liberal causes?

He shrugged. It was impossible to make any sense of what they were doing. They were mentally sick, deranged, filled with pathological hatred.

It was three forty when he pulled into the parking garage behind his office building. He grabbed his attaché case and hurried out, deciding not to upset Dottie by telling her about his encounter with the two thugs.

Dottie greeted him with her usual welcoming smile when he walked in and indicated the thin, white-haired woman seated in the chair across from her.

"Mrs. Pearson is here for her appointment," she said.

Michael managed to produce a smile for Mrs. Pearson, who was suing her husband of thirty-five years for divorce on the grounds of adultery. The adultery was committed with an eighteen-year-old girl who worked for them in the jewelry store they owned. Her husband acknowledged the adulterous relationship with the girl and admitted that the baby she was carrying was his. The girl, now in her fifth month of pregnancy, was three years younger than the Pearson's only child, a boy who was a senior at USC.

"Be with you in just a minute or two," Michael said to Mrs. Pearson.

He stepped into his office and immediately called Lt. Ferraro. He was in luck. Lt. Ferraro had just walked in.

"You'll find this hard to believe," Michael said. "But I just had a run-in with a couple of Carlene Edwards' kidnappers...Not more than twenty minutes ago, in fact."

"You what?" the lieutenant exclaimed.

"I had a run-in with the kidnappers. Two of them. I was coming back from seeing a client at St. Luke's Hospital. They evidently followed me out there, and when I left to come back to my office, they rammed into the back of my car with their car."

"Rammed into you?"

"Yes. Deliberately. On North Allen."

"My God! Were you hurt?"

"No. I was lucky. I had my seatbelt on. Anyhow, one of them was the black-bearded thug I told you about. I'm not sure I told you about the other one, a thin guy with a bald head. Anyhow, I tried to drag the bald-headed guy out of their car...he was driving...and got into a fight with the black-bearded thug. But I couldn't stop them. They got away."

"I don't get it," the lieutenant said. He sounded puzzled. "Why would they do this? It's nutty."

"I can't figure it out either. Maybe it's because I tried to help the Rose Queen and her family. Or because I'm active in the ACLU and some liberal causes they hate. I don't know. It's crazy."

"Did you get their license number?"

Michael felt a bit foolish. "No, I didn't. I just didn't think about it."

"Too bad," the lieutenant said. He sounded disappointed.

They talked a minute or so longer, and then Michael explained that he had a client waiting and ended the call.

For a few moments he sat there at his desk, trying to relax and trying to prepare himself for his session with Mrs. Pearson. Sighing, he got up, opened the door, and smiled out at her.

"Come in, Mrs. Pearson," he said.

Chapter 13

THE PARKING LOT AT CHARLIE'S was filling up fast, the way it usually did Friday evening. Norm and Dottie had driven their own cars, so Michael stood near the backdoor waiting for them.

They pulled in a couple of minutes later, one right after the other, and the three of them walked in the backdoor together.

Ruth had saved a corner booth for them down near the piano, and she waved to them to attract their attention. As they went on down to join her, Michael noticed, surprised, that Jan Ashby wasn't at the piano and wondered where she was.

The booth Ruth had selected was semicircular and large enough to accommodate at least six persons. They ordered drinks and then sat there talking and relaxing and enjoying one another's company.

They had just started on their second round of drinks when Dottie's husband, Bill, came in and joined them. Bill was big and jovial, had thick gray hair, and wore silver-framed glasses that kept slipping halfway down his nose.

Jeannie, the waitress, came over and Bill ordered a gin martini.

"See!" Norm said, shaking his finger at Michael. "Bill's drinking a gin martini just like the rest of us commoners.

Everybody's drinking gin martinis except you, Mike. I suppose if everybody had ordered vodka martinis, you'd have ordered a gin martini."

Michael laughed. "However did you know?"

"I think it's in your genes. I think you were born to be a nonconformist. "

"Hi there, friends," someone said.

Michael turned and saw Larry Augustino coming toward them.

"Greetings, maestro," Norm said to Larry. "Sit down, and I'll buy you a drink."

Michael had always thought Larry looked like Dean Martin. He looked very handsome now in a navy-blue blazer, white shirt, maroon ascot, and charcoal-gray slacks.

"Thanks," Larry said. "But I can't. I'm sitting in for Jan tonight, and I'm a little late getting here. Anything special you folks want to hear?"

Larry, who was in his mid-sixties, had played in most of the better piano bars around San Francisco and LA for the past forty years, but now he was semi-retired and played only when he wanted to.

"I'd like anything by Burt Bacharach," Dottie said, smiling.
"Or anything by Steven Sondheim," Ruth said.

"How about 'Send in the Clowns'?" Norm said.

"I'll go along with whatever they want," Michael said.

"So will I," said Bill.

Larry smiled. "It's always a pleasure to play for special friends like you. Do enjoy yourselves." He made a little bow and left for the piano.

While Larry began playing a medley of Bacharach songs, they ordered another round of drinks. They had just started on them when Norm said, "Well, well, look who's here?" and he nodded toward the bar.

Michael was surprised to see Jan Ashby coming down the stairs. She looked slim and attractive in a dark-red dress, and she looked young enough to be a college student. She waved to Larry Augustino, then saw Michael and the others and smiled and came over to them.

"Hi, everybody," she said.

As the others greeted her, Michael stood up and said, "Care to join us, Jan?"

"I'd love to," she smiled.

He stepped aside so she could sit down, then sat down next to her.

"Larry Augustino said he was sitting in for you tonight," Norm said, smiling at Jan.

She nodded. "We're trading nights. He usually does New Year's Eve, as I'm sure you know, but I'm going to sit in for him that night. His daughter and son-in-law are coming in to visit him for a few days, so he'll be busy with them. Anyway, I came in tonight just to hear him. He's a marvelous performer, and I always learn something from him."

Michael saw Jeannie passing by with an empty tray and signaled to her. She came over and Jan ordered a gin martini.

"See?" Norm exclaimed, turning to Michael with a triumphant expression. "It's now gin martinis over vodka martinis five to one."

"What's this all about?" Jan asked, looking puzzled.

"Oh," said Norm, "Mike here is the only one drinking vodka martinis. All the rest of us are drinking gin martinis, and now so are you. But you know Mike. Once a nonconformist, always a nonconformist."

Jan laughed and patted Michael's arm. "That's part of his charm, what makes him so special."

It wasn't long until they were ordering more drinks. Michael knew he was drinking too much and too fast, but he didn't care. It kept him from thinking about Carlene Edwards and her mother and sister. It even kept him from thinking about Ellen.

They had another round of drinks, and then Dottie and Bill said it was time for them to go.

"Our little dog, Chipper, will think we've deserted him," Bill explained.

"And he needs to be let out and fed," Dottie added.

Ruth looked at Norm. "I think we'd better be going, too, Norm," she said. She turned to Michael. "What about you, Mike?"

"Guess I'd better go, too," he said. "I've got a couple of briefs I want to look over tonight."

Jan put her hand on his arm. "Can't you stay for a little while longer and keep me company, Mike?"

Michael patted her hand. "I'd like to, Jan." His tongue felt heavy from all the vodka. "But I've had a long, hard day, and I do have those briefs to check through tonight, and some work to do in the office tomorrow."

"But tomorrow's Saturday."

"I know. But I have a couple of trials coming up next week that I've got to prepare for."

She looked disappointed, but didn't protest any further.

"I'm sorry you have to work so hard, Mike," she said. "But I really admire you for it."

After the warm, smoky air of Charlie's, the cool, clear night air outside felt good to Michael. As he and the others made their way down toward their cars, he saw two men dart out from between his car and the car next to it. Although the men were only about thirty feet away, he didn't recognize either one of them.

Suddenly there was a huge explosion and a brilliant flash of light coming from the vicinity of his car. Michael instinctively raised his arms to protect his face.

"My God!" he heard Ruth cry.

There was another huge explosion then, and another great flash of light. Michael still cowered there with the others, unable to move, unable to think. And then he realized that the two men he'd seen next to his car were probably responsible for the explosions and were getting away now. He straightened up and saw them running down toward the back of the parking lot.

Without hesitating, he started after them, swearing to himself because all the vodka he'd drunk had turned his legs to rubber. He ran awkwardly down the length of the parking lot, between the rows of cars, shouting at the fleeing men. One of them had started to climb over the brick wall there. The other one swung back toward Michael, a gun in his hand.

Michael threw himself at the man with the gun, slamming him back against the brick wall. The man grunted and swung the barrel of the gun at Michael, grazing his cheek. Michael brought his right forearm up against the man's chin. The man's head smashed back against the brick wall, and he stiffened and dropped his gun.

As Michael lunged for the gun he heard someone off to the side of him. Dropping to one knee, he saw a third man suddenly appear. He got the fleeting impression that the man was big and bearded, then something exploded against the side of his head. He pitched forward, stunned. As he lay there, he heard Norm cry out. He raised his head and through a blur saw Norm and Bill struggling with two or three men. He forced himself to his feet and lurched toward them, then stumbled and fell to his hands and knees.

He got to his feet again and saw the last of the men scrambling over the brick wall. Then he saw Bill lying off to his left, with Norm bending over him. He went over to help them. Bill's nose was bleeding, and his glasses were hanging from one ear. Norm's face was bloody, his tie askew.

Ruth and Dottie came running up to them, white-faced and breathing hard. Several people had come out of Charlie's and were right behind them. A couple of men came up and offered to help them.

"Call the police," Michael blurted.

One of the men said, "We did. They're on their way."

Moments later, a police car swung into the parking lot, red and blue lights flashing, and two officers leapt out.

"What's going on here?" one of the officers demanded. He was tall and muscular and appeared to be in charge.

Michael was still breathing hard. "Somebody blew up my car. Just a few minutes ago."

The officer didn't hesitate. "Let's take a look at it," he said.

They all walked back to look at what remained of Michael's car. Michael was shocked to see the extent of the damage. The body of the car was scorched and ripped and twisted, and all the windows were shattered or blown out. It was clear that some powerful explosives had been planted in or under the car and then somehow detonated.

"It's a wonder the cars around yours weren't destroyed, too," the shorter officer said.

Michael nodded, his face grim.

"Got any idea who did this?" the tall, muscular officer asked. "Or why it was done?"

Michael's eyes hardened. "It's probably the fanatics who kidnapped the Rose Queen a couple of days ago. I was with her when she was kidnapped and tried to help her. Evidently they're out to get me for having become involved in it."

"So you're the attorney who reported the kidnapping."

"Yes, I am. I'm Michael Donovan."

"Well, Mr. Donovan, there isn't much we can do here and now. But we'll cordon off this area, and get someone from our demolition squad out here to see what they can learn. When they're through with this, they'll see to it that what remains of your car is towed off and impounded for closer examination. You can call the department sometime next week and someone in demolition should be able to answer any questions you might have."

Michael hesitated. "I suppose you know Lieutenant Ferraro, don't you?"

The officer nodded. "Oh, yes. I've known and worked with him for years."

"Could you let him know what happened here tonight? He asked me to keep in touch with him and to let him know if anything new related to the kidnapping came up."

"I'll contact him right away," the officer said. His glance took in the others as well as Michael. "Any of you need a ride home?"

"We all have cars here," said Ruth, speaking up in a firm voice. "And we'll see that Mr. Donovan gets home."

The officer took a card out of his billfold and handed it to Michael.

"I'm Sergeant Cope. If you want me for anything, call me at this number. Your insurance agent may want to contact me, for instance."

As the police officers started cordoning off the area around the mangled remains of Michael's car, Ruth turned to him with a sympathetic look.

"Norm or I'll drive you home, Mike."

"Or Dottie or I will," said Bill. "We're much closer to you than Norm and Ruth."

Michael gave them a wry smile. "Thanks," he said. "But I think I'll go back into Charlie's and have a good stiff drink. I could really use one."

Both Ruth and Norm looked disapproving, and so did Dottie and Bill. But Michael didn't care. He really needed a drink.

"Don't worry," he said. "I won't stay long, and I'll take a taxi home."

After they left, he went back into Charlie's to the men's restroom and examined himself in the mirror. He had a bloody abrasion on his left cheek and a lump on the right side of his head that was oozing a little blood.

Stripping off his suit coat, shirt, and tie, he washed the blood off his hands and face and the side of his head, and then gingerly combed his hair. Then he put his shirt and coat back on, and stuffed his tie into his coat pocket. He looked in the mirror. He looked halfway presentable now.

When he stepped out of the restroom, he was surprised to see Jan Ashby sitting at the bar. She was sitting by herself and didn't see him. He walked on over and put his hand on her shoulder. She turned toward him, half frowning, then saw who it was. "Why, Mike." she exclaimed in surprise. "I thought you'd gone home." Her eyes narrowed with concern. "For heaven's sake, what happened to you? To your face and head?"

He shrugged. "I ran into a little trouble out on the parking lot."

"What kind of trouble?" She gripped his arm. "Someone said a car caught fire out there and blew up. Don't tell me it was yours!"

He nodded. "Someone used explosives to blow it up."

"You're not serious."

"I'm very serious. It was totally destroyed."

She looked shocked. "Are you all right, Mike? You didn't have a concussion or internal injuries or anything like that, I hope."

"No, I'm fine, Jan. I wasn't close enough when it exploded to get hurt."

"But why would anybody want to blow up your car?"

"I think the thugs who kidnapped the Rose Queen probably did it. It's probably their idea of revenge because I tried to help her and her family."

She shook her head. "I can't believe something like this is actually happening. It's...it's incredible."

"I know."

Her eyes glinted with anger. "Something's going to have to be done about this. The police or FBI are going to have to catch these monsters...put them behind bars, where they belong."

He nodded.

"What about Norm and the others? You all went out together. Are they all right?"

"Yes, they are. Luckily none of us were hurt by the explosions...actually there were two explosions." He paused. "I didn't mention it, but Norm, Bill, and I did get into a little fight out there with the thugs who planted the explosives. That's how I got cut up, and Norm and Bill got cut up a little bit, too. Unfortunately, though, the thugs got away."

"So that's what happened to your face and head."

He nodded. "I'm afraid so." He saw Dave, the bartender, start toward them to take their order. "I think I need a drink, Jan. Care to have one with me?"

Her eyes softened. "Why don't we get out of here, Mike?...Go to my place? You can have your drink there if you like. It'll give you a chance to relax , and then I can drive you home whenever you want me to."

He hesitated. "I don't want to impose on you," he said.

She put her hand on his. "You won't impose on me at all. It'll be my pleasure."

Chapter 14

Jan swung her red Mercedes coupe up the curving concrete driveway and parked in front of the big brick house.

"Welcome, Mike," she said, turning to him with a smile. "I never dreamt I'd get you out here."

"I never dreamt you wanted to," he said.

She laughed and patted his shoulder. "That shows how little you know me."

The interior of the house turned out to be as impressive as its exterior. The rooms had high ceilings and huge exposed beams, and the furniture was made of carved English oak.

Michael took a quick tour of the oil paintings in the living room. Although he didn't know much about art, he knew what he liked, and he liked what he saw very much.

Jan smiled at him. "Like them?"

"They're wonderful," he said.

"They were part of the estate. You knew my mother and dad were killed in a car accident a few years ago, didn't you?"

"Yes, I'd heard that. It must've been a terrible shock."

"It was. It left me without any family at all." For a moment her expression was wistful, then she shrugged and said, "Getting back to the paintings, the Velazquez and the Van Dyck are originals."

"I don't know which ones they are," he admitted. "They all look great to me."

"I'm glad you like them," she said, smiling. She paused. "Rather than a drink, why don't I fix you something to eat. I bet you haven't had anything since lunch, have you?"

He smiled. "Not since breakfast, in fact."

"Well, then," she said, taking his hand, "it won't take long to take care of that. I don't want any guest of mine leaving here feeling hungry."

She led him down a short hallway and into the kitchen. The kitchen was warm and cheerful with bright red and yellow colors, and with potted plants and copper pots and pans along one wall.

"Now," she said, "let me help you take off your coat so you'll be comfortable." She helped him out of his coat and hung it over the back of a chair. "All right," she said, "what would you like to eat? Name it, and if the ingredients are here, you shall have it."

"What would you like?" he said.

"Forget about me, Mike. You're the one who hasn't eaten all day. How about some scrambled eggs, bacon, and toast?"

"Sounds great," he said.

He watched as she took a white, frilly apron out of the closet across from him, and deftly tied it around her small waist.

"Sit down and relax on one of those chairs there, Mike," she said. "This won' t take long."

"Anything I can do to help?"

"Not a thing, thank you. Just sit there and keep me company." She turned toward the refrigerator, her blonde hair shining under the overhead lights.

Michael pulled a chair back from the table and sat down to watch her. She looked slim and elegant, and she moved about the kitchen with easy grace.

"Won't take long now," she said from where she stood at the stove. "How many eggs would you like?"

"Two would be fine, thanks."

"I'll make that three."

He shrugged and smiled. "All right...he said. "You're the cook."

Although he tried to persuade her to share the scrambled eggs and bacon with him, she refused. Instead, she had a piece of toast with grape jelly on it.

He hadn't realized just how hungry he was until he started eating, and then he had to force himself to slow down. Everything tasted delicious, even the toast and butter.

When they were through eating, they stayed in the kitchen and talked in an easy and casual way over big mugs of aromatic coffee.

"You never mentioned what kind of work your parents did," he said. "Judging from those paintings in the living room, I'd guess they were associated somehow with artists or the art world generally."

"Not really," she said, smiling. "Although art was a passion of theirs, Dad's background and training was anything but that. Dad was a civil engineer and had his own consulting firm. As for Mom, she did major in art in college, but she was quite content to be a housewife and travel with Dad wherever he had to go. Because of the nature of his work, he traveled a great deal and to all parts of the world."

She paused and gave him a mischievous little smile. "Evidently, I know a lot more about you than you do about me."

He pretended to cringe. "Don't tell me you've been digging into my sordid past."

She laughed. "Well, I do know that your dad was a well-known and respected attorney here in Pasadena, and that your mother died of cancer when you were just a boy. And I also know that you and Ellen went to law school together."

He smiled. "You do know more about me, I guess."

Her expression turned serious. "You know I've been married twice , don't you?"

"Yes, I'd heard that."

"Seems I messed up pretty badly, doesn't it?"

He shrugged. "Things don't always work out the way we want them to, no matter how good our intentions."

"Maybe so. But I think I share the blame for the failure of my first marriage. We were just too young to realize what we were getting into. We met our junior year at Stanford and got married midway through our senior year. When we graduated, he joined his dad's stockbrokerage in San Francisco, and I started working at an art gallery only a few blocks away from their offices. My dream was to have a gallery all my own. And it still is. It's my parents' influence, I guess."

"I'm surprised to hear that," he said. "I thought music was the most important thing in your life."

"Oh, it is very important to me. But the graphic arts have been a longtime love of mine. Like Mom, I majored in art in college." She shrugged. "But I've gotten way off the subject. Getting back to that first marriage, we didn't realize at first that we had so little in common. We soon discovered, though, that our interests and values and goals were quite different, and that we were totally wrong for each other. We were like two strangers living together." She paused and gave him an apologetic look. "Hope I'm not boring you, Mike."

"No, not at all."

"Well, to continue this sad little tale, my second marriage turned out to be even worse than the first one. After the first 'one ended in divorce, I took a job playing piano at a small bar in Berkeley. Ever since I was fifteen or so, I'd been playing for social occasions and school events and so on, but this was my first professional job. I met a musician there who had a trio...he played piano, too...and he talked me into singing with them. For a while it was all new and exciting, and we decided to get married. We were both on the rebound, I guess. He'd just gone through a divorce, too. Anyhow, it didn't take long to discover we'd made a big mistake. His big love in life was music, but he also loved to drink and party, and he wasn't at all interested in settling down. And the thought of having children was anathema to him. Eventually we agreed to end the marriage, and I was one depressed and disillusioned gal by then. The good thing, though, is that neither marriage produced any children. It would've been very unfortunate if they had. Broken homes and fathers who don't want to be fathers don't create happy, stable environments for children."

She leaned back, looking at him with a quizzical expression. "You still haven't gotten over Ellen, have you, Mike?"

Her question surprised him. He hesitated. "No, not entirely."

"She's a very smart and attractive person."

"Yes, she is."

She paused. "You haven't been dating anybody since you two broke up, have you?"

"Why, no, I haven't." He shrugged. "I've been too busy even to think about it, I guess."

She reached over and put her hand on his. "Why don't we go into the family room where we'll be more comfortable."

It was cool in the family room, so she lit the gas log in the fireplace, then came over to the sofa and sat down beside him.

"Would you like to marry again, Mike?" she asked. "Or is it too soon to think about that?"

"I guess I haven't though t about that, either," he said. "As I said a few moments ago, I've been just too busy to think of anything except meeting the obligations of our practice."

She slipped off her shoes and drew her slim legs up under her.

"You're not one of those bachelor types who prefer independence to marriage, are you?" she laughed.

He smiled. "Not really. In fact, I liked being married."

He clasped his hands together on one knee. "What about you, Jan? You said you'd like to have a happy marriage and children someday, but do you think you're ready for that kind of commitment now?"

She cocked her head to one side, her eyes twinkling. "Is that a proposal, Mike?" she laughed. She reached up and removed her pearl earrings and put them on the end table. "Seriously, I think I am ready…that is, with the right person. I know I'd enjoy the companionship…the sharing…" She grimaced. "But I'd hate terribly to have another marriage fail. Gads! Two are enough. More than enough. I'm ashamed of that. I don't even like to think about it. I don't think there'd ever been a divorce before on either side of the family."

"But you'd try it again if the right guy came along?"

"Oh, sure. But I'd want to be absolutely positive he was the right one. And then maybe I could have the family I want and also start that art gallery. I think I could do both without neglecting one or the other."

"It's a pretty chaotic world to bring children into, isn't it? "

She smoothed the hair back from her forehead with one hand. "Hasn't it always been?"

"Yes, I suppose so. But the risks are greater now, I think."

She nodded. "You' re probably right. I'm sure our parents never had to worry about random shootings and carjackings and drugs in the schools and things like that."

"I'm sure they didn't."

She put her hand on his arm. "Would you like more coffee?"

"No thanks, Jan. In fact, I think I'd better get going. I've got reams of work to do tonight and tomorrow in order to get ready for trials next week." He stood up and held out his hands. She slipped into her shoes, and he helped her to her feet.

"At least I get to drive you home," she said, smiling.

"Oh, no," he protested. "I'll call a taxi."

"Really, Mike, I want to."

He was keenly aware of her nearness. It would be so easy to put his arms around her, to draw her close, to kiss her full on the lips.

"No, Jan. I won't allow it."

"Please."

"It's very sweet of you to offer," he said, "and I do appreciate it. But it'll be much easier for both of us if I take a taxi."

He left a few minutes later, thanking her for the delicious

bacon and eggs and the pleasant evening, and it wasn't until he got back to his apartment that he realized that all the time he'd been with her he hadn't thought even once of what had happened to his car or what had happened to Carlene Edwards and her mother and pregnant sister.

Chapter 15

At nine o'clock the next morning, Michael went down to the lobby to get the *Times*. He was stunned when he saw the headline on the front page: ROSE QUEEN KIDNAPPERS CONTACT NEWS MEDIA.

Quickly, tensely, he read what appeared below:

> A typewritten letter from the kidnappers of Carlene Edwards, the 18-year-old Queen of the Pasadena Tournament of Roses, was received yesterday at the Los Angeles offices of the *Los Angeles Times* in an envelope bearing a Pasadena postmark of December 27. The letter was signed "White Unity," which is an organization of militant white supremacists who have made themselves known on a nationwide scale over the past year.
>
> The entire text of the letter follows:
>
> *We are holding the Queen of the Pasadena Tournament of Roses captive. We demand that all major newspapers receiving this message print it, in its entirety, on the front page of their next two editions. We further demand that*

all major television and radio networks receiving it present it, in its entirety, on their prime time newscasts for the next two days.

Here, now, is the message:

Attention all white non-Jewish Americans:

The Federal government of our country and all its major means of communication are being taken over by powerful Jewish, academic, and liberal forces which are intent on turning our country into a socialist welfare state. Under their pernicious influence, parasitic and divisive non-whites (blacks, browns, yellows) are sapping the initiative, the strength, and the unity of our society and our capitalistic, free enterprise system and will eventually destroy this country unless stopped by whatever means are necessary.

We implore all non-Jewish white Americans to rally to our cause. Although we are primarily a political movement, our immediate goal is to regain control of our major means of communication, and our ultimate goal is to regain control of our Federal government. If we fail in this, we will lose forever our precious white heritage and our capitalistic way of life, both of which have made us the richest and most powerful nation in the world.

To help us with the costs involved in achieving these two crucial goals, we are demanding a ransom of two million dollars from the officials of the Pasadena Tournament of Roses for the release of the Rose Queen. When and where she will be released, and how and where we want the money delivered, will be explained later this week in another public communication like this.

"Good God!" Michael exclaimed, and shoved the paper under his arm and went back up to his apartment, seething with anger. The idiots who did this were mad…utterly mad!

Suddenly he realized that the phone was ringing in the den.

He hurried in and picked up the receiver, afraid it might be the thug with the black beard or the witch with the masculine voice.

It was Ellen. "Mike," she cried. "I've been so worried about you. It was on the ten o'clock news last night about the bombing of your car. I tried to call you right away...tried several times, in fact. Even after eleven. But you were evidently out."

He felt as if his heart had just done a somersault. "I appreciate your concern," he said, struggling to control his emotions.

She cleared her throat, the way she always did when she was upset.

"I wanted to call you earlier this morning, but a client was coming in on an early flight from San Francisco, and I had to meet her at the airport. Anyhow, thank God you weren't hurt. You weren't, were you? It said on the news you weren't."

"I'm fine, Ellen. We were lucky. No one was hurt."

"It said your car was completely destroyed."

"I'm afraid so."

"I'm so sorry, Mike. Could you use mine? I won't be using it this afternoon."

"Oh no. No thanks, Ellen. Nice of you to offer, though."

"Did you see this morning's paper? About the Rose Queen and the frightening message those madmen sent?"

"Yes, I just read it."

"I didn't see anything about their blowing up your car, though. I suppose it was too late to get it in."

"Probably so."

"My God, Mike, what are those madmen up to? They must be insane, totally without reason or conscience."

"They're psychopaths, Ellen."

"You must feel just awful about all this."

"I do. I feel sick about it."

She cleared her throat again. "Well, Mike, I'm glad I got you, and that you're all right. I do worry about your being mixed up in all this."

"It's a mess, all right."

"I just hope and pray the police catch those monsters before they harm that girl." She paused. "Well, I'd better let you go, Mike. I'm sure you've got lots of things to do, and I have an appointment I can't afford to be late to. If I can be of any help to you, do let me know, won't you, Mike?"

"I will, Ellen. It was sweet of you to call."

He hung up and stood there for several moments thinking about her, wondering whether he would ever be able to get completely over her.

Within the next half hour, he got two more calls. The first was from Norm, who called shortly after ten, and the second was from Dottie, who called only a minute or two after he and Norm had hung up.

Both Norm and Dottie were shocked by the latest news about the kidnappers and their demand for two million dollars. And they both must've been feeling sorry for him because they both invited him over for dinner that evening.

He thanked them, but declined. He knew how valuable weekends were to working couples, and he didn't want to impose on either of them.

Not long after he talked to Dottie, he called his insurance agent and told him what had happened to his car. His agent assured him that his policy would cover the cost of replacing it. Next he called the car salesman who had sold him his Cavalier and informed him that he wanted one just like it, though the latest model, of course. The salesman told him they had a Cavalier demonstrator for sale. It was the current model and had only a couple of thousand miles on it. He would be glad to come by and show it to Michael, he said, and Michael said he'd be glad to have him do so.

While Michael waited for the salesman to come, he received yet another call. It was Jan Ashby.

"Hi, Mike," she said. "I hope I didn't catch you at a bad time."

"Not at all," he said. "I'm glad you called."

"I'll get right to the point," she said. "I was out playing tennis this morning with a friend, and I didn't see the paper until I got back a few minutes ago. Have you seen it yet? The letter from the kidnappers?"

"Oh, yes, I saw it, all right."

"I was shocked. And I know you must've been, too. Is there anything I can do to help? Could you use my car this weekend?"

He felt a twinge of guilt. It was typical of Ellen to offer her car to him. And now Jan had, too.

"It's sweet of you to offer," he said. "But I've already made arrangements to look at a replacement for it. But thanks, anyway, Jan."

"You're welcome, Mike. I know you'd do the same for me. By the way, I want you to know how much I enjoyed last night. I always thought you were a nice man, and last night only confirmed it."

He was embarrassed. "I enjoyed the evening, too, Jan."

"We'll have to do it again, Mike."

"Yes, we will."

"Well, I know you have lots of work to do, so I won't keep you any longer. Do take good care of yourself, Mike, and do let me hear from you, won't you?"

"I will, Jan. Thanks for calling."

He put the receiver back in place, glad she had called. She was a very nice person.

It didn't take Michael long to decide to buy the demonstrator. The price was right, it was just like new, and it was just like his old Cavalier, although it was white instead of red.

After he signed all the papers for it at the dealership, he drove straight to his office. The first thing he intended to do was try to restore those briefs that had burned up in his attaché case in the trunk of his car. Back in law school he'd learned to hang on to all his course notes long after the courses were over, even though the chances of his ever needing them again were rather remote.

And, lucky for him, he still hung on to any and all notes he made for any important aspect of his practice.

After a couple of hours of hard work putting his notes back into acceptable form, he leaned back in his chair, closed his eyes, and thought of the morning's news about Carlene Edwards. It would certainly put a damper on Norm and Ruth's New Year's Eve party, he thought. It was hard to believe it was just two nights away. Thank God it would be a small one. Lots of people and lots of merry-making would be hard to take. Especially now.

He sighed and got to his feet, deciding he needed some fresh air and a cup or two of strong coffee. It took only a few minutes to walk to Benito's, a pleasant little café not far down the street. Before he and Ellen broke up, they used to meet there every now and then for lunch.

The coffee helped. It was hot and fragrant, and as he sat there in the booth sipping it, he became aware of a woman talking in a vibrant way in one of the booths nearby. For some reason, her voice sounded familiar. He tried to place it but couldn't. Funny. He was sure he recognized it, had heard it before. Well, whoever it was, she was talking to another woman whose voice wasn't at all familiar to him.

Although he didn't want to eavesdrop, he couldn't help hearing some of their conversation. It was quite ordinary. They were talking about the upcoming Tournament of Roses Parade, and how busy and crowded Pasadena would be for the next few days.

He finished his second cup of coffee and put a dollar bill on the table for the waitress. As he started to get up, he was surprised to see Ruth Carlson coming through the front door. He raised his hand to wave to her, but she didn't see him and slipped into a booth just up from him.

He smiled. It was his turn now to surprise her. He walked up to the booth to say hello, then stopped. The woman sitting next to her was plump and sandy-haired and looked just like the woman he'd seen with the bald-headed man driving the blue Ford Tempo. There couldn't be any doubt about it. She and the bald-headed man had to be the same couple he'd seen driving past the Edwards' home with the black-bearded thug in the backseat.

Ruth glanced up at him, a surprised expression spreading over her face.

"Why, Mike," she exclaimed. "Where did you come from?"

He forced a smile. "I was in a booth back there having a coffee."

Her surprised expression faded. "Well, I'd like you to meet a couple of friends of mine," she said. She turned toward the plump, sandy-haired woman next to her. "This is Freda Nicholas," she said, and then she nodded at the gray-haired woman sitting across from her. "And this is Edith Carter."

Then she smiled up at Michael and said, "And this is my good and dear friend Mike Donovan, my husband's law partner."

Both women smiled and murmured that they were glad to meet him. And Michael managed to thank them and say that he was glad to meet them, too.

"Care to join us?" Ruth asked.

Michael hesitated. "I'd like to," he said, "but I've got lots of work at the office I've got to get back to."

"Well, that's too bad," Ruth said. "Freda and Edith came down from Santa Barbara for a teachers' meeting yesterday. They both teach English, too. They're driving back home later this afternoon."

He felt awkward and embarrassed. "Well, I'm sorry I can't stay longer," he said. He smiled at the two women. "Do have a safe trip back to Santa Barbara."

The sandy-haired woman smiled. "Thank you, Mr. Donovan. It was nice to meet you." Her voice was deep, almost masculine—like the voice of the woman who had called Thursday night and ranted about the Jews and the colored races.

The gray-haired woman smiled and nodded. "It's been a pleasure, Mr. Donovan."

"It was nice to meet both of you," he said. He turned to Ruth. "See you Monday night, Ruth."

She smiled. "We're looking forward to it, Mike. It should be lots of fun."

He walked over and paid the cashier, troubled over seeing the sandy-haired woman with Ruth. Could she be the same woman he'd seen with the bald-headed man and the black-bearded thug? And if she was, did Ruth know her cohorts and what they were up to? Was that possible?

He frowned and went on out. Maybe he was wrong about the woman. The world was bound to have persons who looked alike and sounded alike. And he knew enough about the unreliability of eyewitness testimony to know how very wrong he might be in thinking that she was the same woman. Cases of mistaken identity abounded. And he knew that very well. Wasn't there even a German expression describing this phenomenon?...*Doppleganger*?

Chapter 16

That evening, Michael put a pepperoni pizza in the oven, then while it was baking, he made and ate a cottage cheese and pear salad. When the pizza was done, he had a couple of pieces of it, then put the rest of it in the refrigerator.

All he wanted to do now was relax and watch something light and entertaining on TV before he got to work on the files he'd brought home with him. He turned on the TV in the den, and kept switching channels until he found an old Fred Astaire and Ginger Rogers movie. He didn't know how long it had been on, but he didn't care.

As he settled back in the recliner, Fred Astaire began to sing George and Ira Gershwin's "They Can't Take That Away from Me." It was a lovely song, and Fred Astaire's voice was pleasant and easy to listen to.

Despite his effort to stay awake, Michael felt himself drifting off to sleep. When he woke up, the Fred Astaire and Ginger Rogers movie was over, and John Wayne was seated on a prancing horse in front of several other men, who were also on horseback.

Michael looked at his watch. Ten thirty. It didn't seem possible. He'd slept over three hours.

He got to his feet and turned off the TV. He'd take a hot, relaxing shower, get into bed, and read through a couple of the files he'd brought home.

As he started for the bathroom, the phone rang. He turned back and picked up the receiver. Who would be calling this late?

"Michael Donovan speaking," he said.

"Hello, Mr. Donovan. Forgive me for calling this time of night. But I couldn't get to a phone till now."

Michael's eyes hardened. My God! It was that woman, that sandy-haired woman! The voice was unmistakable. Husky. Deep. Almost masculine.

"Are you there, Mr. Donovan?"

"What do you want?" he said, trying hard to control his anger. "Why are you calling?"

The woman laughed. "Why to talk to you, of course. Why else?"

It was impossible to be calm. "How long have you known Ruth Carlson?" he demanded, almost choking.

"Known who?" She sounded surprised.

"Ruth Carlson. You were with her this afternoon at Benito's, and don't try to pretend you weren't."

"Really, Mr. Donovan. I don't know what you're talking about. I don't know any Ruth Carlson. And, furthermore, I don't know any Benito's...or whatever you called it. I do know, though, that your partner's name is Carlson. But I don't know any Ruth Carlson. Why? What are you trying to tell me?"

"You don't know Ruth Carlson? You don't know that she's my partner's wife?"

The woman's voice sharpened. "I told you I didn't. How many times do I have to tell you?"

"And you're not an English teacher? You're not from Santa Barbara?"

"Please, Mr. Donovan. I don't have the vaguest idea what you're talking about."

She sounded genuinely bewildered. If she wasn't telling the truth, she'd have to be a psychopath or a pathological liar to lie so convincingly.

"But you are the woman who called me about Carlene Edwards the night before last," he persisted. "Aren't you?"

The woman chuckled. "I was really beginning to worry about you, Mr. Donovan. I was beginning to think you'd slipped over the edge of reason into some kind of paranoid delusion. Of course I called you. I called you Thursday night, to be exact, but before I tell you why I'm calling tonight, I'd like to know whether you read or heard our 'White Unity' message yesterday. It was in all the newspapers and on all the television stations."

He hesitated. "Yes," he said. "I read it in this morning's paper."

"Good. Then you'll be interested to know that we're starting an even bigger media campaign to acquaint every section of the country with our movement, from the smallest towns to the biggest cities. As a matter of fact, we already have a computer network stretching from coast to coast to keep our members informed of our activities and plans. But our goals go well beyond that, of course. We want every thinking non-Jewish white person in the entire country to know about us, about the White Unity movement. We are actively seeking recruits who share our point of view and our convictions. We want them to know what motivates us, what we stand for, what our ultimate goals are. We want to make all of our beliefs and positions a matter of public record. In order to accomplish all this, it's imperative that we have the two million dollars we've asked for for the safe return of the Rose Queen. In fact, if we don't get the entire amount by January 1 of the New Year, we're going to do something drastic to your little black friend. We might even cut off an ear or a hand, for instance. We might—"

"Look," he choked. "How do we know you even have her?...That she's even alive?"

"Oh, come now, Mr. Donovan. Do you think we'd be crazy enough to go to all this effort if we'd already killed her?"

"But..."

"I just thought you'd like to know what we're up to, what we have in mind. If you like, you can run to the police and your ACLU cronies and all your leftist friends and tell them what I've just told you. We'll be delighted to have you help spread the good news." She gave a little snort of derision. "But enough of this. I'm going to say good night now, Mr. Donovan. You'll be hearing from us again before long."

There was the sharp click of a receiver dropped in place.

Michael spent a restless night, sleeping only fitfully, and woke up shortly after nine Sunday morning. He decided to wait until he got to the office to call Lt. Ferraro to tell him about last night's phone call. After all, Sunday was probably the one day of the week the good lieutenant could sleep in.

After toast and coffee, Michael rummaged in the closet for the battered briefcase he'd used back in law school, intending to use it as a temporary replacement for his burned-up attaché case.

When he found it, he stuffed the Zaccaro and Feldman files in it, and left at once for the office.

He didn't waste any time when he got there. He got the latest depositions related to the Zaccaro and Feldman cases out of the file, and had just started to look over the first one when he heard a noise in the outer office. He got up and opened his door, thinking it might be Norm or Dottie.

He was stunned when he saw who it was. It was the black-bearded thug and the red-haired thug who had kidnapped Carlene Edwards. The black-bearded thug stood there with a small black pistol in his hand, and the red-haired thug stood just behind him holding a long-barreled revolver.

"We've brought you something, Donovan," the black-bearded thug said, stepping toward him. "But first get your butt back in your office, and we'll show you what we've got."

Michael flushed with anger but didn't move.

"You heard him!" the red-haired thug said, stepping up beside the black- bearded thug. "Get moving!"

Michael stepped back into his office and turned and faced them, his heart thudding against his chest as the red-haired thug closed the door behind them.

"Come off it, Donovan," the black-bearded thug said. "Don't stand there glaring at us like a madman. We're doing you a favor. We brought you something from that nigger friend of yours." He reached inside his black leather jacket, pulled out a white envelope that had been folded in half, and handed it to Michael.

Michael looked at it warily. There wasn't anything written on the outside of it. It felt quite light, and it seemed to have small, hard objects in it.

"Open it up, for God's sake!" the red-haired thug snarled. "What're you waiting for?"

Suddenly, with a strange kind of clarity, Michael realized that the gun the red-haired thug was waving at him looked just like the Smith and Wesson .357 Magnum that was stolen from Norm's gun collection. The gun was made of stainless steel, was long-barreled, and it had a blue sight with a red streak running down the length of its barrel. That combination of colors was unique, Norm had told him.

"Look!" the black-bearded thug said, his eyes narrowing with impatience. "Open that damn thing up or I'll blow your lousy head off. We haven't got all day, y'know."

Michael awkwardly tore open the envelope and took out the single sheet of paper. Scotch-taped across the top of it were two small gold earrings shaped like rosebuds. He recognized them at once. They had to be the earrings Carlene Edwards was wearing the day she was kidnapped.

With a tight feeling in his chest, he read the handwritten note that appeared below the earrings:

Dear Mr. Donovan,

This is to let you know I'm okay. The people who are holding me captive want you to see to it that the local and national news media are informed of the contents of this note. They don't care how you do it, so long as it's done the very same day you receive this. The news media can verify that I wrote this by checking with my sister Clarice, who knows my handwriting and who had the enclosed earrings made especially for me when I was chosen Rose Queen.

The people holding me will let me go, unharmed, when they get the two million dollars they have demanded. They said if everybody cooperates, they will let me go sometime next week.

In the meantime, they are going to contact the Tournament of Roses officials and tell them when, where, and how to deliver the two million dollars. If they don't get that full amount, they are going to kill me, as well as two other people they say are important community leaders.

Please help me—and them. Our lives depend on it.

Carlene Edwards

P.S. My sister lives in Huntington Beach. Her name, address, and number are in the telephone directory.

Michael looked up from the sheet of paper, his stomach knotted with anger.

"Well," the black-bearded thug said, sneering, "what d'you have to say about that, shyster?"

Michael tried to look calm, to speak calmly. "The police will have to know about this," he said. "They'll have to see the note and the earrings."

The black-bearded thug snorted. "We don't give a damn about the police. Tell them anything you want to. But just be damned sure you tell the news media. They're the ones we want informed."

Michael forced himself to be calm. "I'll talk to the police first, and ask them to inform the news media. They have public relations people who do these sorts of things, and they'll be able to do it faster and better than I can."

"Well, you'd better be damned sure they do!" the black-bearded thug warned. "Otherwise, that little black slut is going to suffer a slow and painful death...and so will a couple of Pasadena big shots we're figuring on picking up if things aren't working out the way we want them to."

"I said I'd take care of it," Michael said, wishing he could smash his fist into that bearded face.

"See that you do, shyster. And I mean right away, the minute we get out of here."

The two thugs left, then, backing out of his office and still brandishing their guns at him. Michael stood there a few seconds, his stomach cramping with anger and frustration. Then he crossed over to the windows and peered down through the Venetian blinds to see whether he could see the two thugs on the sidewalk below. He couldn't see them anywhere.

Going back to his desk, he called Lt. Ferraro's home. He was relieved when the lieutenant himself answered. Michael told him what had just happened, and about the woman's phone call last night.

"How long're you going to be in your office?" the lieutenant asked.

"Till four or five, I think."

"If it's okay, I'll drop by in about half an hour and get the note and earrings."

"All right. By the way, those two thugs were carrying guns that looked just like some that were stolen from the home of my partner. They were stolen the day before the girl was kidnapped, in fact."

"Oh, really? Quite a coincidence. What makes you think they're his?"

"One of them was quite unusual, a Smith and Wesson .357 with a blue sight and a red streak running down the top of its barrel. I'm not sure about the other one, though. It was a small black pistol."

"Did your partner report the theft to our department?"

"Probably. I'm not sure."

They ended their conversation a few moments later, and then Michael called Norm's home. Norm answered and was surprised that Michael had called.

"What's up. Mike? You sound upset."

"I am. Norm. I'm mad as hell. Those two thugs who kidnapped Carlene Edwards just paid me a surprise visit."

"No fooling? Where are you?"

"Here in the office. They brought a note from the girl. It's obvious they forced her to write it. She said they'd kill her and a couple of important people here in Pasadena if they didn't get the two million dollars they're demanding for her release. She enclosed some earrings with the note, the ones she was wearing when she was kidnapped. Said her sister gave them to her and her sister would be able to identify them."

"It's crazy, Mike."

"I know. It's a crazy mess. By the way, those thugs were carrying a .357 Magnum that looked just like the one stolen from you. You know, the blue sight and red streak down its barrel. And they also had a little black pistol."

"You're kidding!"

"No, I'm serious. They were standing only three or four feet away from me. And they were pointing those guns right at me."

"I'll be damned. I don't know about the pistol. But the Magnum sure sounds like mine. I've never seen another just like it."

"I'm quite sure they're yours, Norm. I think those bastards have to be the ones who stole them.

"Sure sounds like it, doesn't it?"

"I talked to Lieutenant Ferraro just a minute ago. He wanted to know if you'd reported they'd been stolen."

"Oh, absolutely. The very first thing." He paused. "Wouldn't it be something if those lowlifes turned out to be the ones who stole them?"

Michael grimaced. "Nothing would surprise me about those guys." He glanced at the stack of files and depositions on his desk. "Well, Norm, I'd better get back to work. But before I let you go, are you coming in tomorrow?"

"Yeah. Sure. I'll be there most of the day, in fact."

"So will I. See you then."

"All right, Mike. Thanks for calling and letting me know about the guns. Sorry, though, about your encounter with those troglodytes."

A few minutes later, Lt. Ferraro came by.

"We'll try to get in touch with the girl's sister right away," he said. "I'll call her as soon as I get to my office, and I'll drive down to see her if she's there. I'd like to have her authenticate the note and these earrings. And then we'll go from there."

Michael's voice tightened with concern. "You'll notify the news media sometime today, won't you? Evidently those degenerates want the news about the girl contacting me out as soon as possible."

The lieutenant nodded. "We'll call a news conference right after we've talked to the girl's sister. And if we can't get in touch with her, we'll still go ahead with one. You can depend on it."

Chapter 17

Dottie was sitting at her desk sorting through some papers when he walked into the office the next morning.

"Oh, Michael," she cried, looking up at him. "I just heard the news a few minutes ago while I was driving in."

"What news?"

"About the girl's note...and those awful men barging in on you yesterday."

Michael winced. So Lt. Ferraro had released the information.

Dottie pushed her glasses back up against the bridge of her nose with one finger.

"Evidently the police didn't give all the particulars," she said. "They simply told what was in the note, and said it was given to you. For heaven's sake, Michael, what happened?"

He shrugged. It seemed as though he was destined to spend the rest of his life telling others about his confrontations with those degenerates who had kidnapped Carlene Edwards.

When he finished telling Dottie what happened, she exclaimed, "Why, they're as bad as those terrorists that've been blowing up airplanes and buildings and murdering innocent men and women and children."

"Yes, they are."

She glanced away for a moment, then turned back, her eyes filling with tears.

"I've had that poor girl constantly on my mind ever since this dreadful thing started," she said in a husky voice.

"We all have, Dottie."

"The police have got to get them, Michael. They've got to get that poor girl safely back."

"Don't worry, Dottie. They will." He tried to look and sound optimistic. "By the way, I thought Norm and I told you to take today and tomorrow off."

She shrugged and indicated the stack of papers on her desk.

"These can't wait, Michael."

"They can wait a few days, can't they?"

She tried to smile. "Never put off till tomorrow what you can do today." Her face sobered. "Before I forget, you had a couple of phone calls just before you came in. Reporters. One from the *Los Angeles Times*. The other from Channel 7. They'll probably call back. And others will be calling too, I imagine. Will you want to talk to them?"

He shook his head. "Tell them I'm not available," he said. He transferred his briefcase to his other hand. "In fact, no matter who calls, just take their names and phone numbers and tell them I'll get back to them as soon as possible."

"What if Lieutenant Ferraro calls?"

"He's an exception. I'll talk to him, of course." He glanced toward Norm's door. "Norm in?"

She nodded. "He came in shortly after I did. Said he talked to you yesterday about those monsters bringing you that note." She frowned. "I just can't get over it, Michael. That poor, innocent girl losing her mother and sister that way, and being held captive all this time."

"It's a lousy situation," Michael said. He shrugged. "Guess I'd better speak to Norm before I get to work. See you later, Dottie."

He walked over and knocked on Norm's door.

"Come in," Norm called out.

Michael opened the door and stepped in. Norm glanced up at him from his desk, his eyes crinkling with sympathy.

"You okay, Mike?"

"Yeah, I'm fine."

"Sit down and chat a minute."

"Thanks, I will." Michael dropped into the nearest chair.

"Those bastards are really bugging you, aren't they, Mike?" Norm said in a voice husky with understanding.

"Yeah, they are," Michael said. "It's the craziest thing that's ever happened to me."

Norm leaned back in his chair. "After you called yesterday, I thought over what you said about those guns. They've got to be mine...at least the .357 Magnum has to be. As I said, I've never seen another like it, and you know how long I've been collecting these things."

Michael nodded. "I know."

They changed subjects, then, and spent the next few minutes talking about the trade infringement case they were working on together. Then Michael went to his office and got to work on the Feldman file. He worked right through the lunch hour, and at one thirty, Dottie knocked on his door.

"I've got something for you, Michael," she said. "May I come in?"

"Of course," he said.

She opened the door and walked in carrying a small paper sack in one hand.

"Better take time out for a little nourishment," she said, handing him the sack.

He opened it, and it contained a cellophane-wrapped cheese sandwich and a big red apple.

"Why, thank you, Dottie," he said, giving her a grateful smile. It's very thoughtful of you. I don't know what Norm and I would do without you."

She shook her head. "I worry about you, Michael. You're going to waste away if you don't start eating properly."

He smiled. "I won't as long as I have you looking after me." He reached for his billfold. "What do I owe you?"

She backed away. "Oh, no, you don't."

"But I insist."

"It won't do any good," she said. She paused. "I'll bring you some fresh coffee in just a minute."

"You're really too good to me, Dottie. You're spoiling me, you know."

"I know," she said, and backed on out and shut the door.

He did as much as he could on the Chapter 11 reorganization he was working on, and then started on a petition for a rehearing before the Court of Appeal. Then he worked straight through the rest of the afternoon drawing up a will and drafting documents for the creation of a trust fund.

At five twenty Norm knocked on his door. "You busy, Mike?" he called out.

"Not if you're the bearer of good news," Michael called back.

The door swung open and Norm stepped in. "Good news I bring you, esteemed partner."

"Oh?"

"Yup. The good news is, my work's all done, and I'm on my way home."

"I mean good news for me, chum."

"Oh...Well, let's see now. How about no news is good news?"

"You'll have to do better than that."

"You're so demanding, amigo." Norm smiled and dropped into the chair across from him. I suppose you know Dottie's been screening calls for you all day. The reporters are hot on your trail, Mike."

"I know. Dottie said they were calling even before I got here this morning."

"Have you heard anything new on the kidnapping?"

"Not a thing. I haven't been out of the office all day, though."

"By the way, we've got to do something about getting Dottie some permanent help. She's swamped with work, Mike ."

Michael nodded. "I'll be sure to talk to her about it before I. leave today."

"Good. That should help brighten her New Year." Norm leaned back and crossed his long legs. "Got a little time to hear something interesting?"

"Sure. I need a break."

"I don't want to impose on you if you're trying to finish up something important."

"You aren't. Believe me. I welcome a break."

Norm loosened his tie. "Well, about an hour ago I got a call from the sister of a young kid involved in an accidental homicide over the weekend. The kid's only eighteen and he accidentally killed the guy he was working for. The guy owns a men's clothing store in LA, and he hired the kid to work for him over the holidays. You probably caught the story on TV or read about it in the paper."

"Yeah, I do remember reading something about it."

"Well, when they closed the store that night…it was last Thursday…the guy made a pass at the kid. The guy was much older than the kid…in his sixties, I think. Anyway, the kid hadn't known the guy was gay, and he tried to ignore him and leave. But the guy persisted in trying to force himself on the kid. The kid gave him a hard shove and the guy fell and hit his head on the counter. It knocked him out cold and put a big gash on his head. He was bleeding pretty badly, I guess. Anyway, the kid panicked and ran out on the sidewalk shouting for help. A couple of cops cruising by stopped and went back in the store with the kid. The old guy had come to by then, and was sitting up. He told the cops that he caught the kid stealing from the cash register and that the kid attacked him. Then the old bastard suddenly keels over and dies. Can you imagine? Just like that. Without another word."

Michael shook his head. "Incredible."

"The kid's in jail now," Norm went on, "because he couldn't make bail. He lives with an older sister, who's divorced and works as a secretary and has a couple of kids under five years old. The sister and the kid are all that's left of the family. The father died of a stroke a few years ago and the mother died of cancer just last summer. Anyway, the kid and his sister are barely getting by financially. It takes about everything she makes to keep her two little girls in day care. But she's willing to pay whatever she can, on a monthly basis for as long as it takes, if I'll handle the case for her brother."

"You agreed to take it, of course."

Norm nodded. "I'd have taken it for nothing."

"I'll help any way I can, Norm."

"Thanks, Mike. I'll probably need some." Norm sighed and stood up, stretching his long arms above his head. "I'll let you get back to work now, Mike. Remember, tonight's the big night. So do come early. The earlier the better. I hate to start drinking all by myself, y'know."

Michael smiled. "I know."

Chapter 18

Michael sat in the living room listening to a Tony Bennett CD and trying to relax. He had mixed feelings about going to Norm and Ruth's tonight. It would be the first New Year's Eve he and Ellen hadn't celebrated together in the past seven years, the last five of those as a married couple.

As he sat there feeling a bit blue and depressed, the doorbell suddenly rang. He got up, sighing, and crossed over to the intercom, wondering who could be dropping by on New Year's Eve. He was surprised to find it was Jan Ashby.

"Hi, Mike," she said. "This is Jan. Did I catch you at a bad time?"

"Not at all," he said. He hesitated, surprised that she had dropped by, that she even knew where he lived. "Come on up. I'll press the buzzer for you."

After he released the door for her, he turned off the CD player, and hurried out to the elevator to greet her. When she stepped out, she looked stunning. She was wearing a simple black cocktail dress with diamond accessories, and carrying a light-weight white coat over one arm.

"Hope I'm not making a nuisance of myself dropping in unexpectedly like this," she said.

"Of course you're not," he said. "I'm delighted you're here."

"I know you're going to the Carlsons' tonight. Are you sure I'm not keeping you from getting ready?"

"I'm positive. I've got lots of time. Come on, Jan. My apartment is just down the hall."

He took her elbow and they started out.

"I just came from visiting a sorority sister of mine," she said. "She got home a couple of days ago after being hospitalized for lung cancer surgery."

"Oh, I'm sorry to hear that."

"I think she's going to be all right now. It was a small lesion on one lung, and the doctors think they got all of it."

"Well, that's good."

"Yes, it's quite a relief. She lives only a few blocks away from here, and after visiting her this evening, I decided, on impulse, to drop by and wish you a happy New Year before going on to work."

"That's very nice of you," he said. He opened the door of his apartment for her. "I'm glad you did."

She stepped in, and he closed the door behind them. "Let me get some more light in here," he said. He crossed over and turned on another lamp.

"I like your decor," she said, looking around her. "It's really very nice."

"Thank you," he said. He stepped over, took her coat, and hung it in the closet next to the door.

As he turned back to her, she said, "That must've been an awful experience for you yesterday."

"Oh, you know about it, do you?"

She nodded. "I heard a brief account of it on the news, but not a detailed report. What happened, anyway, Mike?"

He shrugged. "Not much, really." He didn't want to talk about it, but he didn't want to be rude, either. "The two thugs who kidnapped the girl dropped by my office, made a few threats, and left the girl's note. That's about it." He shrugged again. "Sit down, Jan. Would you like a drink?"

"Thanks, I would. But I can't stay long." She sat down on the sofa. "I'm due at Charlie's in half an hour."

He started across the room to the wet bar. "What'll you have?"

"What're you going to have?"

"A vodka gimlet."

"I'll have one, too, please."

He fixed their drinks, carried them back, and handed hers to her. Then he sat down on the sofa beside her.

She smiled and held out her glass. "May the year to come bring you everything you could possibly want, Mike."

He touched his glass to hers. "Same to you, Jan."

They each took a sip. "When are you leaving for the Carlsons'?" she asked. "You' re sure, now, that I' m not keeping you?"

"I'm sure. As I told you, I've got lots of time before I'm due there."

She gave him a quizzical look. "Are you taking someone? Or is it rude of me to ask?"

"No, it's not rude at all. I'm going alone."

She smiled. "Just see that you leave that way,"

"You have my promise." He smiled back at her.

She put her glass down on the coffee table. "Do you remember the first night we met, Mike?"

"Yes, I do. It was well over a year ago,"

"You asked me to play some Cole Porter songs. Remember?"

He nodded. It had never occurred to him to think of her in a romantic way then. He was in love with Ellen, and nobody else could have begun to interest him.

She fingered the slender diamond bracelet she was wearing. "I remember how shocked I was when I learned about your and Ellen's separation," she said. "I felt so sorry for you. I could see how much you cared for her. And I couldn't help feeling sorry for Ellen, either, because she is a very nice person." She leaned forward and picked up her glass from the coffee table. "I think I'd better finish this and go or I'm going to be late."

She took a sip of her drink, put the glass back down, and started to get up.

"Here," he said. "Let me help you." He got up, held out his hands, and helped her to her feet.

For an awkward moment they stood there, still holding hands.

"I'll get your coat for you," he said, suddenly wishing he could take her to Norm and Ruth's and see the New Year in with her.

He got her coat for her and they stepped out into the hall,

"Oh," she said. "I forgot to tell you. I saw Ruth Carlson this afternoon, and I think she snubbed me. When you see her tonight, tell her I'm a bit upset with her,"

"Are you serious?...about being upset, I mean."

"No, not really." She smiled and they started down the hall. "But I did see her. And she did seem to ignore me."

"Where did all this happen?"

"Downtown. About two o'clock. She was with three men."

"Anyone I know?"

"I don't know," She shrugged. "I've never seen them before, though."

"And she ignored you?"

"Seems that way. They were standing waiting for the light to change. At the corner of Colorado Boulevard and Lake Avenue. The traffic was heavy, and I was stopped right next to them."

"You were in your car?" He pushed the down button of the elevator.

"Yes," she said. "And Ruth couldn't have been more than ten feet away. I honked and waved but she looked right through me and didn't wave back."

The elevator doors opened. "She was probably thinking of something else and didn't see you," he said. He pushed the button for the lobby. "I'll ride down with you."

"Oh, she saw me, all right. She couldn't help seeing me. Maybe she didn't want the odd-looking trio she was with to know she knew me. "

"Odd-looking? "

"Yes, in a way. One was very tall and thin and gray-haired, and looked a lot like Jimmy Stewart. And one had a big mop of bright red hair. And one was really big and husky and had a black beard, and looked like a professional wrestler or football player."

He stared at her, surprised. A mop of bright red hair...big and husky and a black beard...

"What's wrong, Mike? Did I say something that upset you?"

He knew it was pointless to try to tell her his suspicions.

"It's nothing," he said. "I was just wondering whether I might know them."

She looked skeptical. "You sure that's all?"

He nodded, tried to look reassuring. "That's all, Jan."

The elevator stopped and they stepped out into the lobby. She put her arm through his and they crossed over to the big front door and stepped out on the porch. The night air was cool and damp and it was dark now except for the yellowish glow of the porch lights.

He helped her put on her coat and they went on down the sidewalk to where her Mercedes was parked alongside the curb.

"Here," he said. "Let me unlock the door for you." He took her car key from her, unlocked and opened the door, then handed the key back to her.

"Thanks, Mike. And thanks for the drink," she said.

"You're welcome, Jan. I'm glad you dropped by. It was a pleasant surprise."

"Wish Ruth and Norm and the others a happy New Year for me. And do kid Ruth about how miffed I am because of the way she snubbed me."

He nodded and tried to smile. "I will, Jan."

She kissed him lightly on the cheek, then drew back, her eyes shining in the streetlight.

"Come see me at Charlie's, Mike. And do so soon. Or give me a call at home, won't you?"

"I'll do that," he said.

She slipped behind the steering wheel and looked back up at him.

"Happy New Year, Mike. Have a good time at the party."

"Thanks, Jan. And happy New Year to you, too." He closed the car door, then stood there watching as she pulled away from the curb and drove on up the street, her red taillights receding in the darkness.

As he started back up the sidewalk he thought about what she had told him about Ruth Carlson and the three men. Although he couldn't recall ever before having seen the man she described as looking like Jimmy Stewart, her description of the other two—the one with the red hair and the one with the black beard—matched perfectly the two thugs who had kidnapped Carlene Edwards.

He entered the lobby, troubled by this new development. Just what the devil was going on here, anyway? Crazy as it seemed, was Ruth somehow involved with those degenerates who had kidnapped Carlene Edwards?

As he pressed the up button of the elevator, another unpleasant possibility occurred to him. What if the men with Ruth were the kidnappers, and when Jan saw them, they were in the act of kidnapping Ruth and had warned her not to do anything foolish or they'd kill her then and there. Wouldn't that explain why Ruth, who was always so warm and friendly with everybody, had ignored Jan?

The doors of the elevator opened and he stepped in and pressed the button for his floor. And the moment he got to his apartment, he called Norm, praying passionately he wouldn't get bad news about Ruth. The phone rang four times before someone answered it. It was Norm.

"Hey, friend," Norm exclaimed when he heard Michael's voice, "where the dickens are you, anyway? I thought I told you to get here early."

Michael tried to stay calm. "I'm still here at my apartment. Is…is Ruth there?"

"Ruth?…Sure she's here. Where else would she be, pardner? In fact, she's been giving me orders ever since I got home. D'you want to talk to her?"

Michael felt a big surge of relief. "No," he said, relaxing his grip on the receiver. He tried to think of an excuse for wanting to know if Ruth was there. "I just didn't want to come barging in before she was ready for guests."

"Hey," Norm exclaimed. "Didn't I specifically ask you to get here early?"

Michael forced himself to sound cheerful. "That you did, sir."

"Well, then, what's keeping you?"

"Nothing now. But a very beautiful blonde was."

"Har-de-har-har! Don't you wish. Now get your derriere over here, Michael. *Au plus vite*. It's sure as the dickens no fun to start New Year's Eve drinking alone."

Michael laughed. "Be patient, Norman. I'll be leaving in just a few minutes."

He put the receiver back in place. So Ruth was home and evidently all right. What a big relief that was. He shook his head. It still didn't explain, however, what she had been doing with those three men—two of whom apparently looked like clones of the two thugs who had kidnapped Carlene Edwards.

Chapter 19

Norm and Ruth lived on North Kentworth Drive, in a pleasant, secluded residential area of Pasadena. Their two-story home was beige stucco and brick, with dormer windows. It was neat and attractive, and looked like the perfect home for the All-American family.

Michael didn't park in the driveway, but parked instead along the curb out front so he wouldn't be blocked from getting away if he decided to leave early. He locked the car and walked on up the sidewalk to the lighted front porch.

When he rang the doorbell, the door swung open almost at once, and Norm stood there in a brown tweed sport coat and a red bow tie.

"About time, Counselor," Norm said, grinning. "I'm already three drinks ahead of you."

"Oh, no, you're not," Michael protested, stepping in. "I've already had one myself."

"Why, you old rascal, you!" Norm punched him playfully on the arm and closed the door behind them.

"That you, Mike?" Ruth called out from the kitchen.

"Yes, it is, Ruth."

"I'll be out in just a minute."

Michael turned to Norm. "What do you want me to do with this vodka and lime juice?" He held up the paper bag he was carrying.

"Now, Mike. You shouldn't have brought that. We've even got some left over from what you brought last time." Norm turned toward the kitchen. "We'll be in the family room," he called out to Ruth. "Mike's just dying for a drink."

"Ha!" Ruth exclaimed. "I know who's doing the dying."

Michael smiled to himself. Dear Ruth. So bright and vivacious. So kind and good and compassionate. It was absurd to think she'd be involved with those kidnappers. Not knowingly, anyway.

Norm and Michael went into the family room and down to the wet bar. Norm fixed Michael a vodka gimlet and then fixed himself a gin martini. And then he handed Michael his drink and said, "To a happy and prosperous New Year for the firm of Donovan and Carlson. We may be one of the smallest firms in Pasadena, but without doubt we're one of the best!"

"I'll certainly drink to that," Michael smiled.

They touched glasses, and Michael added, "And to our friendship, Norm. I couldn't have a better friend than you."

"Oh, come now," Norm said, pretending to frown. "Let's not get maudlin about it."

As they stood there laughing, Ruth came walking in. "Hi, Mike!" she cried with a warm smile. "Glad you're here." She looked pert and pretty in a long-sleeved white blouse and a maroon skirt. "Norm was making a nuisance of himself out in the kitchen," she said, kissing Michael's cheek. "You know how he likes to snoopervise everything."

"Want me to fix you a martini, honey?" Norm asked, putting his arm around her waist.

She smiled and shook her head. "Not yet, thanks. I've still got some things to do in the kitchen. I just wanted to say hello to Mike here." She patted Norm's shoulder. "Keep your ears open for the doorbell, won't you? The others should be coming along anytime now."

"Don't worry," Norm said. "I'll get there before they get their finger off the doorbell."

Ruth laughed. "Another drink or two and you won't be able to find the front door."

"Now, Ruthie."

"I know. This is New Year's Eve, a time to eat and drink and be merry."

"Couldn't have said it better myself." Norm beamed at her.

"Ecclesiastes," Michael said.

"What?" Norm said.

Ruth smiled. "It's from the Old Testament. Eat, drink, and be merry."

"And also the New Testament," Michael said. "Saint Luke."

Ruth stuck her tongue out at him. "Smarty-pants!" She swung toward Norm. "Now try to behave yourself, my sweet, and go easy on the drinks."

"By the way, Ruth," Michael said. "I'd better tell you before I forget. Jan Ashby said she saw you downtown this afternoon. Said she honked her horn and waved to you, but you didn't wave back."

"Oh?" Ruth looked at him with a puzzled expression. "That's funny. I guess I didn't see her." She shrugged. "I stupidly locked myself out of my car. Some total strangers parked in back of me came to my rescue. The driver had a wire coat hanger in his trunk for just such occasions. It took him only a couple of seconds to get the door unlocked. That must've been when she saw me."

Michael watched her carefully. Her eyes were steady, untroubled. Either she was telling the truth or lying with consummate skill. He believed she was telling the truth. Anyhow, if they were the same men who'd kidnapped Carlene Edwards, they could've been following Ruth, the same way they'd followed him last Friday. If they were crazy enough to follow him that way, then they'd be crazy enough to follow her. Who knew what their intentions were?

Michael smiled at her. "Jan said to tell you she thought you'd snubbed her. She was kidding, of course."

Ruth smiled, her dark eyes glinting. "Well, I hope so."

"She was. She said to wish both you and Norm a happy New Year."

"Well, that's nice." Ruth paused. "You'll have to excuse me now, or I'll never get finished in the kitchen."

After Ruth left, Norm said, "While we're waiting for the others to come, let me show you what I had done to my gun cabinet since it was broken into."

They went into Norm's den, which was just off the family room. It was a cheerful and cozy room with a big oak desk and chair and shelves of golf and tennis trophies. In the far corner was a solid oak cabinet that: displayed all of Norm's handguns. The cabinet was as tall as Norm, and it was almost as wide as it was tall. There were at least thirty expensive-looking handguns on display, all of different sizes and shapes, and there were three empty spaces where the stolen handguns had been displayed.

Michael looked at the cabinet, puzzled. "I don't see anything different," he said. "Looks the same to me...except for the missing guns, of course."

"I had the glass door removed and sliding doors put in," Norm explained. "But I had the guy put in the strongest kind of safety glass you can buy. He said it would take a stick of dynamite to break through it."

"Well," said Michael, "that should protect them, all right." He stepped forward to look at the guns, then turned back to Norm. "I still think it's strange they took only three of them," he said. "You haven't discovered that they took something else from the rest of the house, have you?"

"Not that I know of," Norm said. "At least nothing valuable, or we'd have missed it."

"They must've known you had the guns, Norm. And that' s why they broke in."

"Yeah," Norm said. "It sure looks that way, doesn't it?"

For the next hour Norm was busy answering the doorbell and serving drinks. Dottie and Bill Hunter were the first to come, and it wasn't long until all the others had come, too. They were all old friends of one another. Michael knew they'd be curious about the kidnapping, and he shared what little information he had with them, and that seemed to satisfy most of them.

He didn't know, however, that Norm and Ruth had invited somebody else. He was quite surprised when, a little later, another couple he'd never seen before came along. His surprise changed to astonishment when he realized that the man fitted perfectly Jan Ashby's description of one of the three men she'd seen earlier that day in downtown Pasadena with Ruth. He was at least four or five inches over six feet in height, and he was gray-haired and very thin. And he did look a lot like Jimmy Stewart. In fact, the resemblance was striking. The woman who was with him was rather common looking. She was of medium height and build, and had short brown hair and a thin face.

Norm saw Michael staring at them, and hurried over to him. "They're friends of Ruth's," he explained, lowering his voice. "He's a medical doctor and she's a nurse, and I guess they've been married for quite a long time. Ruth met them a month or so ago through some prof she knows who used to teach at Cal State. Ruth heard him—the prof, I mean—she heard him speak at a seminar last year and was really impressed. Anyhow, she invited all three of them here a couple of weeks ago for dinner. And then she invited all three of them again for tonight's doings. Something came up, though, and the prof couldn't make it."

Ruth brought the new couple over to Norm and Michael, and introduced them to Michael.

"Albert's a physician, an internist, and Claudia's a registered nurse," she said, "and they have a private practice in Glendale."

She smiled at Michael. "And Mike's Norm's partner...you've heard me speak of him...and they've been together over nine years now."

Michael couldn't help staring at the man. He had to be one of the three men Jan had seen that afternoon, the one who looked like Jimmy Stewart. He had to be! He fitted Jan's description to a T.

It was all so bizarre. First, there was the sandy-haired woman Ruth had been with at Benito's. And now there was this tall gray-haired man who evidently was also a friend of Ruth's.

And these two, the woman and the man, were linked somehow to the kidnappers. It seemed incredible. But it was clear what it meant. It meant that Ruth had lied to him. It meant that she did have some kind of relationship with the degenerates who had kidnapped Carlene Edwards.

But what kind of relationship? And why in the world was Ruth, of all people, involved with them?

Chapter 20

Michael watched Ruth move about the room talking to her guests. It was hard for him to believe that she could be associated in any way with the White Unity movement. Not Ruth. She'd never be mixed up in something so crazy, so cruel, so opposed to everything she stood for.

He watched now as she stopped in the center of the room and raised her hand.

"May I have everybody's attention," she called out. "There are refreshments in the dining room for anyone who's interested…roast beef…ham…turkey…cookies…cake…pie…and even more. And it's all there to be enjoyed. So just help your selves."

Norm stepped up beside her. "And for those of you interested in dancing," he said, raising his voice so all could hear, "I'm going to put a Rolling Stones CD on the player to liven up this place and to get you to kicking up your heels."

In a few seconds, the entire room began to resonate with a strident, primitive, repetitious beat. Three of the younger couples began to dance, their bodies twisting, arms flailing, shoulders jerking. Soon they were joined by several more couples. They were all good at what they were doing, and they clearly enjoyed doing it.

Michael turned to Clay and Jennifer Franklin, whom he'd known since law school days at UCLA.

"A little more of this racket that's supposed to pass as music and we'll all be deaf," he said, half shouting.

Clay and Jennifer, who both had fair complexions and auburn hair, looked more like brother and sister than husband and wife.

Clay was with the City Attorney's Office, and Jennifer was with a small law firm in neighboring Arcadia.

Clay, who already had had too much to drink, cupped his hand to his ear and leaned, watery-eyed, toward Michael. "Sorry ol' friend, I didn't hear you."

Michael repeated what he'd just said.

Jennifer gave Michael a knowing and sympathetic look. "I can't stand this kind of music, either, Mike, as you well know."

Dottie and Bill Hunter were standing next to them, talking to the new couple, the Cranes. Clay caught Bill's eye and smiled. "Why aren't you and Dottie out there dancing?" he asked.

"Don't you like the Rolling Stones?"

Bill shrugged. "They're a bit too loud and wild for us, I'm afraid."

"Come on, Jennifer," Clay said. "Let's show Bill and Dottie how to get the ol' blood circulatin'." Clay reached for Jennifer's hands and pulled her out toward the dancers.

Jennifer smiled a little smile of resignation at them over Clay's shoulder, and then she and Clay began to twist, shake, and gyrate with the others.

"Anybody want a drink?" Michael asked. "I'll be glad to fix them."

"No thanks," said Dottie.

Albert Crane shook his head. "None for me, thanks."

"Nor for me, either," his wife said.

"I'd like one," Bill said. "Come on, Mike. I'll join you."

Michael and Bill went over to the wet bar, and Michael fixed himself another vodka gimlet and Bill fixed himself a gin martini.

"I get the feeling the Cranes would rather not be here," Bill said to Michael. "I get the feeling that all this is boring the pants off 'em." He shook his head. "They seem kind of odd, if you ask me."

Michael nodded. "Yes, they do."

"I wonder how Norm and Ruth got to know them."

"According to Norm, Ruth met them through some professor friend of hers who used to teach at Cal State."

The music stopped, and Norm, who was standing next to the CD player, shouted, "Hey, friends! It's time for a change of pace...musically speaking, that is. I'm going to put something on that's a little quieter. Please note I was kind and didn't say 'dull.' Anyhow, it's for those of you who dance to a different drummer, so to speak. So prepare yourselves, friends. Here it comes." He turned and placed a CD on the player. "Here's some of that soporific music from the ancient past, which some of you still seem to like."

A moment later the lovely strains of Glen Miller's "Moonlight Serenade" began to fill the room. Several of the older couples, including Bill and Dottie, moved out to the center of the floor and started to dance.

Michael stood and watched them, enjoying the music and the gracefulness of the dancers. Ellen used to kid him about liking the same music his and her parents had liked when they were growing up. "You're an anachronism, Mike," she'd say, laughing. "You were born a generation too late." And maybe she was right. The music of that time did represent a gentler, more romantic and idealistic way of life.

"Hey, Mike! Why so quiet?"

Michael turned. It was Phil Robbins. He and his wife, Maxine, who were old friends of his, had come over to fix themselves a drink. They were a nice-looking couple, happily married, who had met when they were both students at USC. Phil had been an outstanding quarterback there, and was now a successful insurance executive.

Michael smiled. "I was just enjoying the music," he said.

"It's not bad," Phil said.

"It's beautiful," said Maxine.

"At least you can carry on a conversation while you're listening to it," Phil said. "By the way, Mike, who's going to win the big game tomorrow? Our mighty Trojans or Ohio State?"

Michael laughed. "I hate to admit it, but I think your vaunted Trojans will. They've got the passing and the running backs to pull it off."

Phil grinned. "That's quite a concession, coming from an arch rival Bruin like you. But I've got to admit I think you're right, old buddy."

Phil poured some more gin into Maxine's and his glasses and asked Michael if he wanted his refilled.

"Thanks," Michael said, "but not with that. I'm drinking vodka."

"Then vodka it'll be," Phil said. He picked up a bottle of Smirnoff and started to pour it into Michael's glass.

"Whoa!" Michael protested. "That's too much. You'll have me crawling home at this rate."

Phil grinned. "Wouldn't be the first time, would it, Mike?"

Norm came over and joined them. "It's getting too quiet in here," he said. "I just put something on that will have the whole room jumping." He put his hand on Michael's shoulder. "Do me a favor, will you, Mike? Ruth's in the living room with the Cranes. How about going in there and talking to them so I can drag Ruth out to dance with me?"

Norm and Michael excused themselves and went into the living room. Ruth was sitting in an easy chair talking to the Cranes, who were seated together on the sofa across from her.

"Isn't that music too loud?" Ruth asked, looking up at Norm with a slight frown.

"Too loud?" he said. "It's New Year's Eve, honey, a time for celebration and revelry." He grinned at her. "Anyhow, I came in to ask you to do me the great honor of dancing with me."

"To that?" With a wave of her hand, she indicated the discordant blast of music coming through the doorway from the family room.

"What else, my love?"

Ruth got up, shrugging and smiling at the Cranes. "Excuse us, please." She turned to Michael. "This will give you and Albert and Claudia a chance to become better acquainted. Sit down, Mike. I'm sure the three of you will discover that you have a lot of interests in common."

As Ruth and Norm left the room, Michael sat down in the chair Ruth had just vacated.

Mrs. Crane smiled and said, "Ruth told us that you and her husband have known each other since you were in law school together."

"Yes," he said. "It's been quite a long, time."

"What law school did you go to?" Albert Crane asked. He and his wife both seemed friendlier now.

"UCLA," Michael said.

"I understand it's a good school."

Michael smiled. "I think so. I'm prejudiced, of course."

Albert Crane smiled back at him. "Aren't we all when it comes to our alma mater? Claudia and I both attended Columbia. And that was quite a long time ago, too, wasn't it, Claudia?"

She grimaced in a humorous way. "Do you have to remind me?" No one spoke for a few seconds. Michael tried to think of something to say.

"Will you take in the Rose Parade tomorrow?" he asked.

Mrs. Crane glanced at her husband. "We might watch some of it on TV," she said. She looked back at Michael with a wry expression. "But parades are all so much alike nowadays, aren't they? If you've seen one, you've seen them all."

Michael nodded. "Yes, that's true."

She smiled. "I must admit, though, I do like seeing the horses. They have some simply magnificent ones each year, don't they?"

"Yes, they do," said Michael, thinking that anybody who liked horses couldn't be all bad.

He turned to Albert Crane, deciding on impulse to see whether he could catch him off guard.

"By the way," he said. "It was certainly fortunate for Ruth that you could help her with her car this afternoon. You must be pretty handy with a coat hanger."

Albert Crane didn't say anything for a moment. "I'm afraid I don't know what you're talking about, Mr. Donovan," he said, his eyes narrowing.

Michael tried to speak casually. "Ruth locked herself but of her car this afternoon. In downtown Pasadena. I thought she said you and a couple of your friends helped her get it open with a coat hanger."

Albert Crane looked puzzled now. "I think you must've misunderstood her. I couldn't possibly have helped her. I was nowhere near Pasadena this afternoon. In fact, I was in Glendale and busy with my patients." He looked and sounded very convincing.

Michael shrugged. "Sorry," he said. "Evidently I did misunderstand her."

They talked about a variety of things, then, the weather, the economy, and trade relations with Japan. They were just about to run out of conversation when Ruth came hurrying back in looking red-faced and disheveled.

"Well," she gasped, "that should take care of Norm for a while." She took a deep breath and looked at them expectantly. "Now, tell me. Did the three of you find something interesting to talk about?"

Michael got to his feet. "Yes, we did. We had a very nice talk." He paused. "Would you care to sit down, Ruth?"

She shook her head. "No thanks, Mike. I think I can catch my breath better standing up."

He smiled at her, deciding to try to carry through with her the little ploy he'd already tried unsuccessfully with Albert Crane.

"While you were gone," he said, "I told Dr. Crane it was nice of him and his friends to help you get your car unlocked this afternoon."

Ruth's smile disappeared. "You what?"

"I told Dr. Crane that you said he helped you get your car unlocked this afternoon."

Ruth looked upset now. "How in the world did you get that idea, Mike? I told you I didn't know who it was who helped me. They were total strangers."

Michael tried to look apologetic. "Sorry, Ruth. I guess I just wasn't listening carefully. I must've had my mind on something else."

Ruth looked a bit mollified. "Well, it's easy enough to do, I suppose." She straightened the collar of her blouse. "Anyhow, what are you doing calling Albert 'Doctor'?" she demanded. "You should be on a first-name basis by now. All three of you. Isn't that right, Claudia?"

Mrs. Crane smiled and nodded. "Absolutely."

Albert Crane stood up. "I think Claudia and I could use another drink," he said. He held out his hands and helped his wife to her feet. Then he turned to Ruth and Michael. "What about you two?"

"Good idea," said Ruth. She gave Michael a wry smile. "Come on, Mike. I think we could all use a drink."

Chapter 21

Michael glanced at his watch. Midnight was only a few minutes away now. The men were standing near the wet bar, and the women had gathered down by the fireplace.

Suddenly Michael realized that, somewhere in back of him, Ruth Carlson was calling out his name. He turned toward her.

"Mike!...Oh, Mike!" she was crying as she hurried toward him. "You're wanted on the phone."

Michael looked at her, surprised. Who the devil would be calling him here at the Carlsons'?...And now of all times? Surely not those degenerates who'd kidnapped Carlene Edwards.

"Who is it, Ruth?" he asked, stepping toward her.

Her face looked pinched, worried. "It's Ellen," she said.

"Ellen?"

"Yes. I think something's wrong. She sounded terribly upset."

Michael's chest tightened with fear. "What did she say?"

"She just wanted to talk to you. I think she's been crying. She's on the phone in the kitchen."

Michael hurried out to the kitchen. The receiver was on the counter, where Ruth had left it.

"This is Mike," he said, picking it up. "What's wrong, Ellen?"

"Oh, Mike, I'm so glad I got you."

Ruth was right. Ellen had been crying.

"Tell me what's wrong, Ellen."

"I'm...I'm in a terrible mess, Mike." She sounded scared, about to panic. "I hate to ask, but could you come and get me?"

"Where are you?" he asked huskily.

"San Marino. At...at a party. I sneaked in this bedroom to call you." Her voice broke. "I'm afraid, Mike. He's high on drugs and he attacked me...hit me."

"Hit you! Who hit you?"

"Ron."

"Ron?" He almost choked on the word.

"Ronald Putnam. You know."

He felt a sudden, wild anger. "For God's sake, Ellen. Get out of there. I'll meet you out front. Give me your address.

"Oh, God, I don't know what it is. We're someplace on Rosalind Road, south of Cal Tech. It's a big white stucco house...with two wings and big white pillars out front."

"I've got to have the address, Ellen. Are you at Putnam's home?"

"No. We're at the McLindens'. Douglas McLinden. He's a friend of Ron's. His name must be in the telephone directory. I'd look it up, but there isn't a directory in here."

"Hold on a second. I'll look it up." He put the receiver back on the counter, grabbed the telephone book next to it, and rifled through its pages. There it was!...Douglas A. McLinden...Thank God he was listed. The address was 3900 Rosalind Road.

He dropped the telephone book back on the counter and picked up the receiver.

"Ellen?...I found it.... Now listen carefully. Get your coat...or whatever you've got with you...and get out. Get out any way you can. Go out the back door if necessary. When you do get out, hide out front somewhere...behind a tree or shrub or something...so you can see the street. I've got a new car now. It's just like the old one. Only it's white. I'll turn the fog lights on so you'll know it's me. Is that clear?"

"Yes, Mike. For God's sake, please hurry!"

"I'm leaving right away. I should be there in about twenty minutes,"

He dropped the receiver back in place. So that dirty bastard Putnam had hit her! No telling what kind of craziness was going on there.

He hurried back to the family room. Ruth was standing just inside the doorway waiting for him.

"Is she all right?" she asked, her eyes wide and fearful.

Michael nodded. "I think so. She's at a party and evidently it's turned rough and she wants to get out of there. I'm taking off to get her. Sorry about this, Ruth."

Some of the fear left her eyes. "Why don't you bring her back here. Mike? We'd love to have her."

"I don't think she'll feel up to it, Ruth. She's pretty upset." He paused. "I'll slip out without saying anything to the others. Make up some kind of excuse for me, if you have to. Thanks for everything. Ruth. Sorry to have to leave like this."

It was cold outside and getting foggy. He turned on the overhead light and reached in the glove compartment for the new street guide he'd bought.

He scanned through its pages, found Rosalind Road, and then found that part of the map showing where it was. He quickly decided how to get there, then turned off the overhead light and pulled away from the curb.

When he reached Colorado Boulevard, he was surprised to see how empty and deserted that part of it looked. He'd expected to see some signs of preparations for the Rose Parade tomorrow. He drove on down to California Boulevard, then turned west toward Cal Tech. A couple of minutes later he was turning south on Rosalind Road.

He switched on his fog lights and drove slowly along, watching both sides of the street for the house Ellen had described—a big white stucco house with two wings and big white pillars out front. In the fog and darkness, it was impossible to make out house numbers.

He drove another two blocks south, then saw, off to his right, what must be the house he was looking for. The porch was all lit up, and it looked as though all the windows on both floors were lit up, too. There were a dozen or so cars parked along the curb, and several more cars parked in the big U-shaped driveway out front.

He pulled over and parked several feet back from the last car at the curb, leaving his fog lights on. Then he got out and peered up at the stretches of lawn and shrubs and trees on both sides of the driveway. He couldn't see Ellen anywhere. He swore to himself. Surely she'd gotten out of there by now.

He waited a minute or two longer, his stomach knotting with worry, then started up the driveway. As he hurried past the Mercedes and Jaguars parked there, the heavy *thump thump* of music coming from the house grew louder. And when he got close to the porch he was relieved to see the numbers 3900 above the big double doors. No doubt about it. This was the right place. But where the devil was Ellen?

He paused and looked around him. What to do now?

He glanced at his watch. 12:25. She should've been out of there at least half an hour ago.

What could be wrong?

He half ran back down the driveway to his car and stood there, worried, frustrated, afraid to think of what might be happening to her.

He waited there several more minutes, then decided he'd waited long enough. He was going to have to go in the house to find her.

He hurried back up the driveway. Whoever saw him when he walked in would probably think he was one of the guests. If the hosts saw and challenged him, he'd just say that Ronald Putnam had invited him to drop by for a drink.

He opened the big double doors and stepped in. The *thump thump* of electronic music was coming from an open doorway in the wing off to the left of him. In front of him, a flight of stairs curved upward to a second floor. Off to his right, in the other wing, was another open doorway.

He hesitated, then crossed over to the room where all the music was coming from and looked in. It was a big room with a high ceiling and crystal chandeliers, and it was jammed with people dancing in a wild, frenetic way. The deafening, discordant music came from the far end of the room where several long-haired musicians pranced about with their gaudy guitars.

Michael was almost positive Ellen wouldn't be there. But he wanted to be sure. Who knew what Putnam, high on drugs, might force her to do? When he was sure she wasn't with the wild partyers there, he went back across the foyer to the open doorway in the other wing and looked in. It was a big rectangular room, and there was the pungent odor of marijuana in the air. A number of people were gathered together in small groups, smoking and drinking and talking. Some were seated, some standing.

After looking about the room, Michael felt sure Ellen wasn't there, either. He looked at the couple standing a few feet away from him. They appeared to be about his age, though perhaps a few years younger. They would have been nice looking if they hadn't looked so dissipated. The man was wearing a handsome dark-blue suit, and the woman, a pretty pale-green dress that showed off her voluptuous figure.

Michael walked over to them. "Pardon me," he said. "Do you happen to know Dr. Ronald Putnam?"

The man blinked in a vacant, disoriented way. "Dr. who?" he said, wetting his lips with the tip of his tongue.

"Dr. Putnam," Michael said. "Dr. Ronald Putnam. He's a medical doctor, an orthopedic surgeon. He practices here in Pasadena. He was here not more than half an hour ago with a pretty, dark-haired woman."

The man blinked several times and rubbed his eyes with the back of one hand.

"Afraid I don't know anyone by that name," he said., slurring the words. He turned to the woman with him. "Know who he's talking about, babe?"

The woman looked at Michael. The pupils of her eyes were large and unfocused.

"Haven't the foggiest idea," she said in a hard voice.

Michael didn't bother to thank them. He turned and hurried back out to the foyer, wondering what to do next. He could either go up the stairs nearby or down the hall to his right. He hesitated, then moved quickly down the hall. There was a closed door at the end of it. He paused a moment, then turned the doorknob and pushed the door open.

Except for a lighted floor lamp across the way, the room was dark. At first, he didn't think anyone was there. And then he saw a man and a woman standing close together near a big desk at the end of the room. They were embracing, and the woman's dress was pushed up around her hips. Michael couldn't see them very well, but he could see the woman wasn't Ellen.

He stepped back out, closed the door, and stood there, tense and frustrated. Where the hell was Ellen? Could she be somewhere upstairs? Could Putnam have found her in that bedroom she called from and prevented her from leaving?

Chapter 22

Two couples crossed the foyer going toward the room where the dancers were.

"Pardon me," Michael called out, hurrying up to them. "I' m looking for Dr. Ronald Putnam. Do you know him?"

One of the women, a blowzy-looking redhead, spoke up, her eyes glinting with amusement.

"We sure do. Matter of fact, last time I saw him he was going up those stairs in back of you...with another man and some woman. A *ménage a trois,* no doubt. You'll probably find them in one of the bedrooms up there."

Michael's stomach cramped. "Thanks," he blurted, then turned and ran toward the stairs, then up them. A long hallway stretched out to the right of him, with several doors on each side of it.

He ran to the first door to his left and pushed it open. The only light in the room came from a small lamp on a dresser across from him. He saw two persons lying close together on a bed next to the far wall. Their arms were locked around each other and their clothes were halfway off.

He backed out, repelled. They were men. One looked old enough to be the father of the other.

He ran across the hall to the first door on that side and pushed it open. The overhead light in the room was on, and there were several men and women struggling with one another, red-faced and panting, on a big round bed. Two of the women were bare breasted and stripped down to panties. Two or three of the men were stark naked. The nose of one of the men was bleeding. No one was smiling or laughing, and there was a lot of grunting and cursing going on.

Michael winced. Good God! The whole place was full of deviates!

He whirled around and ran down the hallway to the next door to his right. He pushed against it, but it wouldn't open. He put both hands against it and pushed as hard as he could. The door moved back, but only an inch or so. Someone must've shoved a chair or something heavy up against it.

Ellen! Maybe Ellen had barricaded herself in!

He hesitated, then knocked on the door, calling out her name. There was no response. He knocked again, harder, calling out her name several times. Still no response. Then he thought he heard someone crying. It sounded like a woman.

He put his shoulder up against the door and shoved. Hard. The door moved back a few inches. He shoved again, even harder. The door didn't budge. He moved back a couple of steps and then rammed up against the door. The door burst open, and a chair that had been shoved up against it went skidding off to one side.

He stepped on in. The room was dark except for a strip of light under a closed door across from him. He paused there, waiting for his eyes to adjust to the darkness.

Suddenly he heard muffled crying sounds coming from somewhere to his left. He glanced in that direction. In the faint light from the hallway, he could make out someone stretched out on a bed in the corner. He clenched his fists and stepped toward whoever it was.

His throat tightened and he had to fight to keep from crying out. It was Ellen. She was lying naked on her back, a gag of some kind stuffed into her mouth, her wrists and ankles tied to the bedposts.

As he bent over her, the room exploded with light. He spun around. The door across the way had swung open. A naked man stood there. For a moment, Michael froze where he was.

My God! It couldn't be! He must be hallucinating.

"Hey!" the man croaked. "What the hell you doing here?" Michael charged toward him, slamming his shoulder into the man's gut. The man fell backward, and Michael drove him on into the bathroom. The man grabbed him around the neck with one heavily muscled arm and jerked him off balance.

Michael reached out for something to hang onto. The man brought his knee up in a short, powerful arc, catching Michael in the groin and sending him back against the sink. Michael struggled to his feet. The man struck out at him with his fist and caught Michael on his left temple, stunning him. The man swung again, striking him on the side of his head and sending him spinning back against the toilet. Michael ducked under the man's next blow and brought his fist up with all his might. He caught the man flush on his chin, and the man fell backward and dropped to the floor.

Gasping for breath, Michael stared down at him. He couldn't believe it. It didn't seem possible. What in the world would the black-bearded thug who'd helped kidnap Carlene Edwards be doing here?

Michael shook his head, confused, bewildered. But maybe it wasn't the thug. Now that he could see the man this close up, he didn't look as big or as tall as the thug, and his beard didn't look as black.

So it had to be just a coincidence that they looked so much alike. That was probably it. A coincidence.

Michael turned, his mind reeling, and ran back into the bedroom to Ellen. She was gagged with her own bra. He struggled with the knot, got it undone, and pulled the bra out of her mouth. She choked and started to sob.

"It's all right," he said, breathing hard. "Hold on a couple of seconds and we'll be out of here."

He could see now what that bearded bastard had done to her. Her lower lip was swollen and bleeding and there was an abrasion on one cheek and bruises on her upper arms.

Her wrists and ankles were tied to the bedposts with pieces of her slip and panty hose. He untied her, careful not to hurt her, and helped her to a sitting position on the edge of the bed.

"Think you can walk all right?" he asked.

She nodded and wiped the tears from her eyes with her fingers.

"I'll be all right," she choked.

Her dark-blue dress lay crumpled on the floor next to some men's clothing. He helped her to her feet, steadying her, then picked up her dress and handed it to her.

"Better put this on," he said.

She slipped into the dress, which was ripped down one side, and he zipped up the back of it for her.

"Where're your shoes?"

"I don't know," she said huskily. She looked about her with a dazed expression.

He saw the dark-blue heel of a woman's shoe sticking out from under the end of the bed. He stepped over, got the shoe, and found the other one next to it. He handed them to her.

"Is he dead?" she asked, her voice trembling. "It sounded as if you were killing each other."

"He's all right."

She slipped into her shoes. "Ron's in there, too."

"What?"

"Ron. Ron Putnam's in there, too. In the bathroom. Passed out. That man you fought with carried him in there to turn the shower on him. Ron's loaded with drugs. Both are."

Michael crossed quickly over to the bathroom, stepping over the unconscious body of the bearded man. The door of the shower stall was partly open. He saw Ronald Putnam huddled in the corner, on the floor. He was leaning back against the wall, his head slumped against his chest. He was naked and his wavy brown hair and tan, muscular body were glistening with beads of water.

Michael forced himself to reach down and feel Putnam's neck for a pulse. His pulse was strong and steady. Michael straightened up and turned to go.

Ellen stood in the doorway, her eyes wide with fear. "Is he all right?"

Michael nodded. "Still unconscious, though."

She glanced at the bearded man, who still lay where he'd fallen. Michael could see by the rise and fall of the man's chest that he was breathing all right. He'd probably be coming to any second now.

Michael stepped over to Ellen and took her arm. "Do you have a coat?"

"Yes. Downstairs." Her voice was calmer. She seemed to have control of herself now.

"Let's get out of here," he said.

He guided her through the bedroom and out into the hallway. The hallway was empty. They moved on down it and on down the stairs, with the heavy beat of music still coming from the wing where the dancers were.

Ellen's coat was in a cloakroom under the stairs.

"Did you bring a purse?" he asked.

She nodded. "A small one. It's here in the coat."

He helped her slip into her coat, a simple dark-blue one that he'd always liked on her, and they turned and started for the big double doors that would take them out of the house.

Chapter 23

"I'll turn on the heater as soon as the engine warms up," Michael said, pulling away from the curb.

Ellen sat huddled away from him, looking down at her lap. She drew her coat closer to her, but didn't say anything.

He made a U-turn at the end of the block and headed back up Rosalind Road. He felt sick about what had happened to Ellen. And he was still shocked that Putnam and that bearded man, whoever he was, would attack her that way. And he was especially shocked that Putnam would.

He turned on the heater and they drove along for several more blocks without speaking.

Suddenly, in a low voice, Ellen said, "I'm so ashamed…so ashamed." Then she began to cry.

He'd never seen her like this before. She'd always had firm control over her emotions. He reached over and put his hand on hers, wishing there were something he could do or say to help her feel better.

He waited until she had stopped crying, then said, "I think we'd better report this to the police, Ellen."

She swung toward him, looking upset, her eyes still red and tearful.

"Oh, no, Mike! I don't want to do that."

"But..."

"Please, Mike. Not the police."

"But those bastards shouldn't be allowed to get away with this."

"Please, Mike!" Her voice rose sharply.

He hesitated. "All right, Ellen. Whatever you want."

She took a handkerchief out of her purse and dabbed at her eyes.

"Anyhow," she said in a husky voice, "they didn't accomplish what they wanted to. They didn't rape me...if that's what you're thinking."

He stared at her. For a moment he didn't grasp what she had said. And then a great sense of relief flooded through him. Thank God for that!

She dabbed at her eyes again. "It was all so crazy," she said. "Ron got me upstairs on the pretext of showing me some...some renovations the McLindens had made on the second floor. I hadn't ever met the man who was with us before...the one you fought with. He's a friend of Ron's, some kind of engineer, I think. Anyhow, both of them were high on methamphetamine or crack or something. But up until then they'd been behaving all right. Then, when they got me up there, Ron caught me by surprise...stunned me, really...saying he and his friend wanted to have sex with me. I told him he must be out of his mind, and started to leave. We were in the hall then, and he shoved me up against the wall and hit me in the face."

Michael gripped the steering wheel, cursing Putnam under his breath.

"It was awful, Mike," she said after a moment. "I'd never seen Ron like that before. He was like some other person...hard and mean and rough. And it was absolutely crazy what he asked me to do. Why, I'd never even come close to being intimate with him. Had never given him any reason to believe I would or wanted to. Anyhow, he and that bearded man dragged me into one of the bedrooms near the top of the stairs.

"It was full of half-dressed people, and I managed to twist away and run into the hall. I was afraid they'd catch me going down the stairs, so I ran the other way and hid in the first room I came to. Luckily, they didn't see me. Anyhow, that's when I called you. I was just beginning to feel safe after I hung up when they came storming in. They'd evidently been searching for me. Ron was like a maniac. He started hitting me, then threw me on the bed, and he and that bearded bastard started ripping off my clothes. I fought as hard as I could, but they were just too big and strong for me. They tied me to the bed and gagged me, and then they took off their clothes and...and suddenly Ron keeled over and passed out. Then that bearded imbecile said he would stick Ron under a cold shower to bring him to, and come back and show me what a real man could do. He carried Ron into the bathroom, and that's...that's when I heard you calling out my name." She choked and started crying again.

Neither of them said very much in the remaining time it took to get to Ellen's place on Euclid Avenue. Michael found an empty parking space on the street out front, and moments later they were taking the elevator up to her apartment on the fifth floor.

When they got inside, he helped her take off her coat, and she hung it in the closet next to the entryway.

"Thank you, Mike," she said, turning back to him with a sad little smile. "And thank you, too, for all your help tonight. I hate to think what would've happened to me if you hadn't come to get me." She rose on her toes and kissed his cheek. "I'm so sorry I spoiled your New Year's Eve."

"I'm just glad I could help."

"You *will* stay awhile, won't you? I'd appreciate it if you would."

"You sure?"

"Yes. I'd rather not be alone right now." Her eyes began to fill with tears.

He put his hand on her shoulder. "I'll stay as long as you like, Ellen."

"Thank you, Mike."

"I don't like to mention this," he said, withdrawing his hand, "but Putnam might try to call you when he comes to his senses. You'd better be prepared just in case he does call."

She grimaced. "God, I hope he doesn't. If he does, he'll just have to talk to my answering machine. I'm never going to speak to that man again. Not ever!" She shrugged and pointed toward the entryway. "You can use that bathroom just off the entryway if you want to tidy up." She smiled wryly. "You do look a bit beat up, you know." She brushed a strand of hair back from her forehead. "I'm afraid to see how I look. If you don't mind, Mike. I'll slip into my bathroom and take a quick shower."

"Take your time," he said. "I'm in no hurry."

"When you're through tidying up," she said, "fix yourself a drink." She indicated the liquor cabinet in the corner. "Or if you like, there's coffee in the kitchen. Just help yourself to whatever you want."

"Thanks." he said. "Coffee sounds good to me."

The bathroom off the entryway was done in silver and gold, and handsomely appointed. Its big, wide mirror told him he looked pretty bad. His tie was pulled halfway down, and the breast pocket of his blazer was ripped almost all the way off. A couple of buttons were missing from his shirt, and his right cheek was scratched and swollen, and he could see a bruise starting to form there.

Stripping to his waist, he washed his hands and face, and then combed his hair. Then he put his shirt back on and went back into the living room, and draped his blazer and tie over the back of a chair.

The only coffee he could find in the kitchen was Instant Sanka, so he put a pot of water on the stove to heat, and in a couple of minutes he'd prepared a cup of hot coffee. He took the coffee back out to the living room and sank into one of the easy chairs and tried to relax.

He still couldn't believe what had happened. My God, Ellen was a highly moral, highly intelligent woman. Just what the hell did those two bastards think they were doing, anyway. They both had tried to rape her, for God's sake!

"Oh, there you are!" Ellen said, coming into the living room. "Good! I see you made yourself some coffee."

Michael smiled and got up. She looked like a different person. She wore a pale-blue dressing gown that he'd never seen before now, and her hair was brushed back from her forehead and she'd put on just a trace of lipstick.

"Would you like some coffee?" he said. "I've got some water heating on the stove."

"I'd love some."

They went into the kitchen and he fixed her coffee for her. It gave him a funny feeling to be with her like this. They were both being a bit formal with each other. It was as though they'd never been husband and wife. He couldn't help feeling a sense of regret, of sadness.

"You're going to spoil me with all this attention," she said with a faint smile.

In the bright light of the kitchen, he could see that her swollen lower lip was actually cut, and that she'd powdered over the abrasion on her cheek. It made him mad as hell all over again to see what those bastards had done to her.

"Are you hungry?" she asked. "I could put something together in just a minute or two."

"No, thanks, Ellen. Coffee's all I want. But if you're hungry, go ahead and have something."

She shook her head. "Coffee's all I want, too."

They went back out to the living room, and sat there sipping coffee and talking.

"I'm still shocked by what happened at the McLindens'," she said with a rueful expression. "Always before, Ron had been a perfect gentleman, warm and thoughtful and considerate."

"Did you know he used drugs?"

"No. No, I didn't. I knew a few friends of his did from time to time. But I'd never known him to do so. I was actually stunned when I saw what was going on at the McLindens'."

"You said earlier that you'd never met that bearded friend of his before. Do you remember his name?"

She frowned. "No, I don't. Ron introduced him to me only a few minutes before we went upstairs. I'd been talking to the McLindens, and he brought him over to introduce him. I'm not sure, but I think the man's name was Morrison and that he was some kind of engineer. Aeronautical, I think. I think he'd come to the party alone." She gave Michael an apologetic shrug. "I'm so sorry I dragged you into this, Mike. It's such an awful mess."

"I'm just glad we were able to get you out of there, Ellen, and that you're all right."

Her eyes filled with tears. "Good old Mike. You'll never change. I do love you, you know. And always will."

His throat tightened. "I love you, too, Ellen."

"Well," she said, with false cheerfulness, "enough of that. Would you like more coffee?"

He reached over and put his hand on hers. "First, I think we'd better discuss what you intend to do about what happened tonight."

"I don't know what you mean. Mike."

"Look, Ellen. I know it isn't pleasant for you. But you're going to have to do something about this. Those bastards shouldn't be allowed to get away with what they've done. Would you like me to help you file criminal charges? Institute a civil action?"

She frowned and withdrew her hand. "Really, Mike, I don't even want to think about anything like that. All I want to do now is try to forget everything about it, block it out of my mind. Anyhow, there are lots of other things I've got to think about now, very important things."

"Listen, Ellen. You're a lawyer. You—"

"Please, Mike. I meant what I said."

He started to argue with her, then realized it would be futile to do so.

"All right," he said, shrugging. "It's your decision, Ellen."

"Anyhow," she said, "I've got something important to tell you. I wasn't going to say anything about it until I'd definitely made up my mind. But after what happened tonight, I think I'd better tell you."

"Tell me what, Ellen?"

"Last week I received an offer to join a very good law firm in Washington, D.C. Miller, Silverman, and Norton. You may have heard of it. Anyhow, Charles Miller, the head of the firm, contacted me about a month ago on a visit out here and talked to me about joining them. He made it sound very attractive. I'd come in as a partner and at almost double what I'm making now. And I'd get to concentrate on environmental law, something I haven't been able to do very much of here, as you know." She paused and smiled. "Well, Mike, what do you think of that?"

He was stunned. He didn't like the idea at all. Washington, D.C.! Why, it was three thousand miles away. My God, he might never see her again.

"Are you going to accept?"

She leaned back with a wan smile. "After what happened tonight, I think maybe I'd better."

He didn't stay very long after that. He could see that she was tired, and so was he. They said good night at the door, and he kissed her on the forehead. She hugged him and said, "Thanks for everything, Mike. Thank you with all my heart. You'll always be very special to me, and I'll always love you. I want you to know that."

Chapter 24

THE NEXT MORNING HE SKIMMED through the *Times*, looking for something new on the kidnapping. But he didn't find anything. He glanced at the foreign and national news, and had just turned to the sports section when the phone rang.

It was Norm Carlson.

"Morning, Mike," Norm said cheerfully. "I'm calling to wish you a happy New Year and to find out if Ellen's okay. Ruth told me about the call you got from her last night."

"Thanks, Norm. Happy New Year to you and Ruth, too. As for Ellen, she's just fine. The guy she was with last night zonked out on drugs, so she needed a ride home. That's what that was all about."

He didn't think it would be fair to Ellen to tell Norm more than that, and Norm knew better than to ask.

"Well, I'm glad she's okay, Mike. By the way, I still have those extra tickets for the game today, and Ruth is still insisting that I ask you to take in the game with us."

Michael winced. The thought of fighting all that traffic to and from the game, and then sitting in a crowded and noisy stadium all afternoon wasn't at all appealing to him.

"It's nice of you and Ruth to ask," he said, "but I think I'll just stay here and relax a bit. And then, later on, I have a lot of work to do that I simply can't put off doing."

"You sure? We'd love to have you, Mike."

"Thanks, anyway, Norm. But I do need to rest a bit before I get to work on the stuff I brought home."

"Well, I'd better keep this short. Ruth has some things she wants me to do before lunch. But before I hang up, are you going to the office tomorrow?"

"Yeah. I'd better."

"Well, see you there. I've got some work to attend to, too. Take care, my friend."

"You, too, Norm. Thanks for calling and for the offer to take in the game with you. And thank Ruth for me, won't you?"

"I will, Mike."

"Oh, yes. And thanks, too, to both of you for the great party last night."

"'Twas our pleasure, Mike."

After Michael hung up, he decided he might as well get started on the files he'd brought home, and then rest and relax later on. As he opened his briefcase, the phone rang. He leaned over and picked up the receiver.

"Michael Donovan speaking," he said.

"Happy New Year, Mike," Jan Ashby said. Her voice was bright and cheerful. "Are you surprised I'm calling?" She laughed. "Or maybe you don't recognize my voice."

He laughed, too, pleased that she'd called. "Of course I recognize your voice. I'd recognize it anywhere. And happy New Year to you too, Jan."

"Thanks, Mike. If you're wondering why I called, I decided I wouldn't spend the day with those friends of Mother's I told you about the other night, the ones at Newport Beach. And since I'll be all alone today, I thought I'd call you and see if you'd care to join me for lunch and watch the big game on television. I can stick some chicken breasts and potatoes in the oven, make a salad, and prepare some kind of dessert. Is that enough to tempt you out of your hermitage?"

He chuckled. "Sounds very tempting, Jan. And it's very nice of you to ask. But I've brought all this work home and—"

"Now, Mike. It's New Year's Day. Can't it wait?"

He hesitated. It would be nice to see her, to spend the afternoon with her. He could use some cheering up.

"All right," he said. "I'd like to come."

"Wonderful!" she said. "How would two or two thirty be?"

"Either would be fine."

"Make it two, then. The sooner the better. Now, I'd better let you go before you change your mind. Goodbye, Mike." She laughed and hung up.

He felt a bit guilty about accepting her invitation after turning down Norm and Ruth's. But he was sure they'd understand. And it would certainly be a lot better than fighting all that traffic and sitting in a jam-packed Rose Bowl all afternoon.

She must have been looking for him through one of the front windows. For no sooner had he rung the doorbell than she opened the door and exclaimed, "I'm so glad you're here, Mike."

"I'm glad to be here," he said, returning her smile and thinking how pretty she looked. Her blonde hair was loose about her shoulders, and she was wearing a long-sleeved lavender silk blouse and tailored black slacks and black sandals.

She closed the door behind them and turned toward him. "Oh," she said, looking at his face and frowning. "You're hurt."

"It's nothing," he said.

She stepped up to him, put her hand gently to his chin, and turned his face toward the light from the window.

"Your cheek is all bruised," she said. "Don't tell me you had another fight with those awful kidnappers."

He shrugged, not wanting to lie to her or seem evasive. "I got into a scuffle last night with some guy who was high on drugs.

He wasn't anybody you or I know, and it was a situation I couldn't avoid." He shrugged again. "If you don't mind, Jan, I'd rather not talk about it."

Her expression softened. "All right. Mike." She paused. "Come join me in the kitchen. I think the chicken's about ready to come out of the oven. Are you hungry?"

"Yes, I am."

"Good." She put her arm through his and guided him down the hall and into the kitchen. The kitchen smelled appetizingly of baking chicken and freshly baked dinner rolls.

"If you like," she said, "we can carry our plates into the den and eat and watch the game there. Or we can eat here in the kitchen or in the dining room and then watch the game a little later. What's your pleasure, Mike?"

"It's up to you, Jan. Let's do whatever is easiest for you."

"Well, it'll probably be easier to eat here in the kitchen. Everything will be handy and we can relax and talk and enjoy ourselves. Then, as I said a moment ago, we can watch the game later in the den."

"Sounds good to me," he said.

He thought the dinner was delicious. The chicken breasts and dinner rolls and baked potatoes and tender green peas were very tasty, and the lettuce-and-tomato salad with sliced cucumbers and radishes and Thousand Island dressing was very tasty, too.

When they finished, he smiled across at her. "Everything was perfect." he said. "It couldn't have been better."

"Why, thank you, Mike. Are you ready for dessert?"

"I am, if you are," he said.

They had chocolate and vanilla ice cream with chocolate chip cookies, and then, using the same mugs they'd used the other night, they had hot and fragrant coffee. By the time they'd had their second mugful, neither of them felt much like watching the football game.

"It's so nice out," she said, "maybe we should take a little walk before we see what's happening in the Rose Bowl. Would you like to, Mike?"

"Yes, I'd enjoy it."

She laughed. "At this rate, we're going to miss the whole game."

"I don't mind," he said, "if you don't."

They left the house and walked down the shady street. There were attractive homes and well-kept lawns and shrubs and trees on each side of them. The entire neighborhood was quiet and pleasant and peaceful, and it gave Michael a good feeling to be there. It was almost like being back in the neighborhood around North Grand Oaks where he'd grown up as a boy, except that the homes there had been much more modest.

By the time they had gone several blocks, they were holding hands and she was telling him how she'd always loved dogs and cats and had had them as pets when she was growing up, and that she'd finally decided, after thinking about it for a long time, to get herself a little dog, and she was going to do so sometime within the next few weeks, even though she knew it would probably tie her down a lot.

"What kind will you get?" he asked, pleased to learn that she liked dogs and cats because he'd always liked them, too.

"Oh, any kind or any mixture, I suppose. It really doesn't matter. I plan to get one at the dog pound. They have to destroy so many, you know. It's dreadful to think about, isn't it?"

He nodded. "It's terrible."

"By the way," she said, "guess what I'll need after I get the dog." She gave him a playful smile. "And I don't mean a dog leash or a doghouse, though I'll probably need them, too."

He laughed. "I don't know what else you'd need. Do you mean a veterinarian?"

"I'll probably need one of those too," she laughed. "But that isn't what I had in mind. What I'll need is a little boy or a little girl."

"A little boy or girl?"

"Yes. To go with the dog. Every dog needs a little boy or girl, and every little boy or girl needs a dog. Right?"

He smiled. "Don't tell me you're planning to adopt a child."

"Oh, no…though that's not a bad idea. What I have in mind is something else…something more basic." She looked at him, her eyes crinkling humorously in the sunlight. "But enough of this bantering. We'd better hurry back, Mike, or we'll miss the whole game."

They sat on the sofa in front of the big television set at one end of the den. The Rose Bowl was crammed with people, and the stands were a brilliant and colorful mosaic in the late afternoon sunlight.

According to the sportscaster, the game was now halfway through the third quarter.

"USC has the ball on Ohio State's 40-yard line," the sportscaster was saying, "and is leading Ohio State by…Hey," he exclaimed, "what's going on here, anyhow?"

Michael looked at the sportscaster, surprised at the sharp tone of his voice.

"There's an airplane up there," the sportscaster cried, "and it's sweeping down over the stadium! What is this, anyhow? Someone's taking a very foolish risk."

A camera had focused on the airplane. It was a small single engine monoplane, and it was diving down over one end of the field. It was no more than thirty feet above the turf, and the camera lost it for a moment, then caught it again.

The airplane rose in a sharp, steep climb over the far end of the stadium, performed a tight turn, and swept back down over the field again, this time at a higher altitude, perhaps sixty or seventy feet.

"Whoever's flying that must be crazy," Jan exclaimed, sitting stiffly forward on the edge of the sofa. What in the world is he trying to do?"

Michael shook his head. "I've no idea."

"There's real confusion down on the field," the sportscaster shouted. "The airplane has dropped what appears to be a small parachute, and the referees have halted the game. Yes, I can make it out now. It *is* a small parachute...not much bigger than a man's handkerchief...and it's floating down toward mid-field. There's something hanging down from it, but I'm not sure what it is."

Jan turned to him with a puzzled look. "What do you suppose that's all about, Mike?"

Michael watched in disbelief as the small parachute settled down somewhere near the 30-yard line on the other side of the field. Another camera had picked up the flight of the airplane, and it was now high in the sky and disappearing toward the San Gabriel Mountains.

Jan turned to Michael with a puzzled look. "What do you suppose that's all about, Mike?"

Michael shrugged. "Some kind of prank, maybe. It looks like something those Cal Tech kids might've cooked up. They're always trying something funny or daring like that."

The camera was on the two sportscasters in the broadcasting booth now. The balding one named Ken was speaking to the gray-haired one named Lee.

"Well, Lee, this is all mighty strange. It's certainly a first for me, anyway. I guess all we can do now is wait until our color man Bill Woodward tells us what he's found out about that parachute."

A dark-haired, athletic-looking young man appeared on the screen. He was standing on the sideline on the other side of the field holding a mike in one hand. His face looked grim.

"Hello, Ken," he said. "This is Bill Woodward down here on the sideline. The police have now taken charge of that little parachute that was dropped by that airplane a couple of minutes ago. I'm afraid what I have to tell you isn't at all pleasant. In fact, it's pretty bad. Evidently a plastic bag was attached to the parachute and two human hands were found inside it. The hands were cut off at the wrist and...Well, it's all pretty gruesome, but the hands appear to be those of an African-American woman. One of the policemen said there was a note in the bag along with the severed hands. Evidently it's from a white supremacist organization called White Unity. The policeman refused to give any further information, except to say that the nature of the note was threatening."

Chapter 25

He left Jan's at ten after seven. When he pulled into the driveway of' his apartment house twenty minutes later, the sky was already turning dark. He started to insert his plastic card in the metal box to open the garage door when something suddenly clamped down hard on his wrist.

"Don't move, shyster!" someone said in a harsh voice.

Michael recognized the voice at once. It was the black-bearded thug.

"Now," the black-bearded thug said, "move over!" He released Michael's wrist with one hand and shoved a gun up against Michael's ear with the other.

Michael's chest tightened with fear. He tried to think of some way to resist.

"Move!" the thug said, opening the door. Or I'll blow your goddamn head off!"

As Michael started to move over, someone tapped on the back window of the other side of the car. It was the red-haired thug.

He was holding the same long-barreled handgun he'd been carrying Sunday. He motioned to Michael to unlock the back door on that side.

The black-bearded thug climbed in behind the steering wheel and pointed his small black handgun at Michael.

"Open the door for him," he said, nodding his head toward the red-haired thug.

Michael reached back and released the lock. The red-haired thug opened the door and climbed in.

"Behave yourself, punk," he said, poking the barrel of his gun up against Michael's neck. "My finger'll be on this trigger every second of the way now."

The black-bearded thug shifted into reverse and backed out of the driveway. Then he turned north toward Colorado Boulevard. In the streetlight across from them, Michael saw a blue Ford Tempo pull a few feet away from the curb and then pause there. It looked like the same blue Ford Tempo he'd seen at least three different times now, the one driven by that bald-headed creep. Evidently he was waiting for them to pass on by.

Michael turned and looked at the black-bearded thug with a sick feeling beginning to spread through his gut. He realized now that the man had to be the same one who was with Ronald Putnam last night and had helped attack Ellen. He had to be. The resemblance was too great to be coincidental. What had confused him last night was that he'd never dreamt he'd see him there, and especially in those circumstances. And then when he did see him, naked and bare-footed like that, he'd looked so different, so much smaller.

But how the devil was he linked to Ronald Putnam, a prominent Pasadena medical doctor? And what kind of relationship existed between the two of them and Ruth Carlson?

"You haven't gone to sleep on us, have you?" the black-bearded thug said, glancing over at Michael with a little sneer.

"No. I haven't," Michael said as calmly as he could. "I'm just wondering what this is all about. What is it you want with me?"

"You'll find out soon enough," the black-bearded thug said, slowing down as they came to an intersection.

The red-haired thug spoke up in back of him. "Didja see the big game in the Rose Bowl this afternoon, shyster?" he asked with a scornful laugh. "Or were you too busy trying to get into that songbird's panties?"

Michael clenched his fists but didn't say anything.

The red-haired thug slapped the barrel of his gun against the back of Michael's head.

"I'm talking to you, you dumb bastard!"

Michael bit down on his lip to fight the pain, but still didn't say anything.

"Listen, smart ass," the red-haired thug said. "You know why I'm asking. You saw what that plane dropped on the football field, didn't you?"

Michael turned and faced him. "Yes, you dirty bastard," he said. "I know what—"

The red-haired thug slammed the gun barrel down against Michael's left ear. Michael had to clench his teeth to keep from crying out.

"Listen, you son of a bitch!" the red-haired thug said in a harsh voice. "Don't go playing tough guy with me!"

Michael forced himself to sit up straight, to keep his hand away from his ear. He wasn't going to give that lousy bastard the satisfaction of knowing he'd hurt him.

The black-bearded thug glanced at Michael with a little smirk.

"Better watch what you say, shyster. My friend's got a helluva temper."

The post-game downtown traffic was still heavy. The black-bearded thug slowed down at the intersection of Madison and Colorado, and turned west on Colorado. In the side-view mirror on his side of the car, Michael saw the blue Ford Tempo following close behind them.

The black-bearded thug noticed that he'd seen it. "Saw our friends back there, did you?" he said. "Well, don't go fooling yourself into thinking the cops are going to spot it and save your ass. Because they're not. We're much too smart for that, shyster. That's a new set of plates on it. In fact, we've got new plates on all our cars."

They crossed Fair Oaks Avenue, still going west on Colorado. Both the thugs were quiet now. It worried Michael that they weren't trying to keep him from seeing where they were going. Could this mean they were planning to kill him?

He glanced at the black-bearded thug, who was watching the traffic up ahead, his big face impassive.

"I suppose you know that holding me against my will like this is a federal crime," Michael said.

The black-bearded thug turned toward him with a derisive look.

"Oh, my!" he said. "How very thoughtless of us. Do you think you can ever forgive us for this?"

"Federal crime is it?" the red-haired thug chortled from the backseat. "Just what the hell difference do you think that makes to us?"

They crossed the Arroyo Bridge, turned under the Ventura Freeway, and headed north. High up in the darkness to their left, Michael could see the lights of the big, expensive homes that dotted the steep and craggy hills there. Where the devil were they taking him? he wondered, his stomach tightening with fear.

Suddenly the black-bearded thug braked hard, and made a sharp left turn. Michael saw the headlights sweep over a wooden bench between two giant palm trees at the corner, and then move on up the street. As they headed up the hill, Michael looked for street signs, but couldn't make out any names in the darkness. In the rearview mirror, though, he could still see the headlights of the blue Ford Tempo following along not far behind them.

They circled upward for a few minutes, and finally reached the top of the hill. As they drove along its curving ridge, they passed several big homes behind big walls and ornamental iron gates.

Suddenly the black-bearded thug turned into a driveway to the right of them. At the end of the driveway, illuminated in the moonlight, was a big pale-pink stucco house with a red tile roof. It looked like a palace to Michael. It was three stories high, and most of the big draped windows on the first floor were lit up. There was a big four-car garage set next to the house, with brightly lit pole lights at each end of it.

As the black-bearded thug drove on up the driveway, Michael noticed an outside stairway on the side of the garage next to the house. He presumed it led up to servants' quarters on the second floor. He also noticed a car parked off to the right of them in front of the farthest garage. It was a dark red four-door Buick sedan. He couldn't help wincing. It had to be the car that was used to kidnap Carlene Edwards.

The black-bearded thug stopped Michael's car in front of the garage nearest to the house and got out. The red-haired thug got out, too, and opened the door next to Michael.

"Okay, punk," the red-haired thug said, brandishing his gun at Michael. "Get your butt out of there!"

As Michael climbed out, the blue Ford Tempo that had been following them drew up alongside them and stopped. The bald-headed creep who was driving it climbed out, and so did the two men who were sitting in the backseat. One of the men was Albert Crane, the tall, thin medical doctor who, along with his wife, had been at Norm and Ruth's New Year's Eve party. The other man was Ronald Putnam, the orthopedic surgeon Ellen had been going with, who, with the black-bearded thug, had tried to rape her last night.

Michael's stomach cramped with anger. So Putnam was mixed up in this crazy mess, too. And Michael's dear friend Ruth had lied about that incident in downtown Pasadena with Albert Crane and the black-bearded and red-haired thugs.

It was hard to believe. Incredible, really. What strange kind of conspiracy was this anyway?

Chapter 26

"Follow 'em, stupid," the red-haired thug said, shoving the barrel of his gun up against Michael's back.

Michael winced and fell in behind Albert Crane and Ronald Putnam, both of whom had deliberately ignored him since getting out of the car. As he followed them up the sidewalk, they passed a lighted water fountain with a beautiful bronze statue of a water nymph poised gracefully in the center of it.

Every step of the way, the red-haired thug stayed close behind Michael, and the black-bearded thug and the bald-headed creep strayed close behind both of them.

They went on up to a large, covered front porch, and Albert Crane took a ring of keys out of his hip pocket, unlocked the big front door, and walked on in. As they followed him into the spacious oak-paneled entrance hall, Michael was surprised to see Albert Crane's wife, Claudia, come hurrying toward them from the back of the house. She was wearing a light-blue blouse and gray slacks. She glanced at Michael with cold, haughty eyes, as though he were an intruder whom she'd never seen before.

"Any problems?" she asked her husband.

"None," Albert Crane said. "Is everything quiet up there?"

She nodded. "Everything's under control."

Michael tried not to stare at her. Her whole manner was different from what it had been last night at Norm and Ruth's. She looked remote now, detached, like a robot.

The black-bearded thug looked at Albert Crane. "Want him taken up right away?" He indicated Michael with a wave of his thumb.

Albert Crane nodded. "Go ahead. Dr. Putnam and I will be up shortly."

The black-bearded thug turned to the red-haired thug. "Let's go," he said. He started toward the flight or stairs to their right.

The red-haired thug prodded Michael's back with the barrel of his gun.

"Get movin'!" he said.

Michael followed the black-bearded thug up the first flight of stairs, with the red-haired thug only a step behind him. Down below, he saw Albert Crane and the others disappearing from the entrance hall into the back part of the house.

The black-bearded thug didn't stop on the landing of the second floor, but went on up to the third floor where a carpeted hallway stretched out to either side of them. He paused there and turned back to Michael with a sly smile.

"Want to see something interesting?" he asked.

Before Michael could reply, the black-bearded thug said, "Follow me," and turned and started down the hallway to their left.

"You heard him," the red-haired thug said, and prodded Michael with the barrel of his gun.

Michael followed the black-bearded thug with an uneasy feeling in his gut. They passed a closed door to their left and a closed door to their right, and then, down near the end of the hallway, the black-bearded thug stopped.. There was a closed door on each side of them. The black-bearded thug unlocked the door to their right with one of the keys from a leather case he was carrying, and stepped in.

The red-haired thug prodded Michael in the back with his gun.

"Go on, punk. Get in there."

The only light in the room came from a small brass lamp on a dressing table across the way. The red-haired thug prodded Michael another step forward, and Michael saw the bed then. It was an old-fashioned four-poster. It was in the opposite corner and someone was in it.

Suddenly he felt cold allover. It was Carlene Edwards. She was lying on her back, her eyes closed. There was a gash on her forehead and both her eyes looked bruised and swollen. A blanket was drawn up over her arms and chest, and a rumpled comforter lay at the foot of the bed. She looked dead.

The black-bearded thug glanced at Michael with a cruel smile.

"Surprised?" he asked.

Michael tried to speak but couldn't. He felt sick to the stomach.

The black-bearded thug stepped up to the bed, bent over, and placed his fingers on the side of Carlene's neck.

"She's had a heavy dose of sedatives," he said over his shoulder. He straightened up and turned back toward Michael.

"Doc Crane gave them to her a couple of hours ago. He said she wouldn't be waking up for a good long time."

Michael swallowed hard, still shocked at seeing Carlene there, but relieved to know she wasn't dead.

The black-bearded thug laughed. "You look like you just got a good, hard kick in your balls, shyster. What's the matter? Didn't you expect to see the little slut alive?"

Michael clenched his fists, his stomach twisting with pain.

"Maybe you'd like to see just what a great surgeon old Doc Crane is," the black-bearded thug said in a syrupy voice. He bent over and. pulled the blanket and the sheet down to Carlene's knees.

Michael's eyes glazed over with emotion. Carlene lay there in a white bra and a white half slip. Both arms were at her sides. For a dizzying moment he couldn't believe what he saw. Her hands were still there! Both of them! They hadn't cut them off!

My God! What kind of hoax was this? What kind of sick, perverted mind would dream up something like this?

The black-bearded thug, who was watching Michael's stunned reaction, threw back his head and laughed harshly. The red-haired thug joined in, cackling behind him.

"Snookered you, did we, shyster?" the black-bearded thug choked.

Michael stood there. Unable to think. To speak.

"We snookered everybody," the black-bearded thug chortled. "Everybody in that stadium. Everybody watching on TV. The whole damned country. And it was easy, shyster. So damned easy, thanks to Doc Crane."

"Tell him," the red-haired thug said, smirking. "Tell him how old Doc did it."

The black-bearded thug looked at Michael, still chortling.

"Yeah," he said. "A shyster like you oughta get a big kick out of this. What Doc Crane did was cut off the hands of some nigger whore who'd overdosed on drugs. She was in a funeral home in LA that was owned by a friend of his. After they cut off her hands, they closed up the casket and nobody was the wiser.... Oh, come on, now, shyster. Don't look at me like that. We're not stupid, you know. We know the cops will have those hands checked out by some experts. We know they'll find out they've been had. But that way we keep everybody guessing...wondering what the hell is going on. Keep 'em off balance, so to speak."

Michael stared at him, sickened by what he'd heard. The man was psychotic. Had to be. They all were!

"Let me tell you something else, shyster," the black-bearded thug said. "We..." He glanced toward the door, his voice trailing off.

Albert Crane and Ronald Putnam stood in the doorway. "What the hell's going on here?" Albert Crane demanded, scowling. "You were supposed to put him down there with the other two."

The black-bearded thug looked sheepish. "I thought he'd like to see his little slut girlfriend first...see how you snookered everybody with that nigger whore's hands."

"You talk too damned much," Albert Crane said, his voice trembling with anger. He indicated Carlene Edwards with a wave of his hand. "Cover her up for God's sake. We don't want her getting sick on us. We've still got plans for her, remember?"

The black-bearded thug turned and drew the sheet and the blanket back up over Carlene's chest and shoulders. She still lay unmoving, still deep in sleep.

"Now," Albert Crane said, with a curt nod toward Michael, "get him down there with the other two. And make it fast, for God's sake!"

Chapter 27

Michael followed the black-bearded thug down the hallway with the red-haired thug once again right behind him. They passed the stairs from the entrance hall and went on down the hallway. They passed two doors. The one to the left was closed and the one to the right was partly open, and Michael could see that it was a utility closet containing cleaning appliances and supplies.

They continued down the hallway, and the last door to their right was closed, and so was the last door to their left. The black-bearded thug opened the door to their left, and the red-haired thug jabbed Michael with the barrel of his gun.

"In you go, punk." he said.

Michael stepped in, and the black-bearded thug and the red-haired thug followed right behind him. Michael stopped and looked around him. They were in a large bedroom with handsome furnishings. A man with a droopy mustache stood at the back of the room. He was in shirtsleeves, and Michael could see a pistol showing above the waistband of his trousers.

"They behaving themselves?" the black-bearded thug asked the man with the droopy mustache.

The man nodded. "Can't do much else. I made damned sure of that."

"Well," the black-bearded thug said, "let's get this idiot in there with them. You got enough cord left?"

"Yeah, I think so," the man said. He crossed over to a small writing desk along the wall to their left. The desk had a large roll of what looked like white plastic clothesline cord on it. Next to the roll of plastic cord were a couple of rolls of black electric tape and a roll of wide adhesive tape.

Michael looked at the black-bearded thug. "Before you do anything to me," he said, trying to keep his voice calm, "I want to know why you've brought me here."

The red-haired thug looked at the black-bearded thug and started to snicker. "You'll find out soon enough," the black-bearded thug said. The man with the droopy mustache came walking over to Michael with the rolls of plastic cord, electric tape, and adhesive tape. He put the rolls of tape on the floor and started to bind Michael's wrists behind him with the plastic cord. He was very thorough, and just as he tied the last knot, Albert Crane and Ronald Putnam walked in the door.

Michael looked at Albert Crane and said, "I don't know what you intend to do with me. But if you're really a friend of Ruth Carlson, let the Edwards girl go. She's just an innocent teenager, for God's sake! She hasn't harmed anybody. Keeping her here won't do any good. Let her go and keep me instead. Use me for publicity or to help get the two million dollars or for anything else you want. I'll say or write anything you like. Just let the girl go."

The red-haired thug started to snicker again, and the black-bearded thug started to snicker, too.

Albert Crane frowned at them, "Knock it off, you guys!" he said. He swung toward the man with the droopy mustache. "You better finish tying him up in the closet."

The man looked at Michael with small, hard eyes. "Okay," he said. "Head for that closet over there." He put one hand on Michael's back and shoved him toward a door that was partly open on the far side of the room.

Michael stumbled, then regained his balance, and walked around the king-size bed toward the door. The man with the droopy mustache stepped around him and pulled the door all the way open.

Michael saw that it was a well-lighted walk-in closet. At first, he didn't see anything but clothes hanging in a row on each side of it. And then he saw them. A man and a woman. They were seated at the back end of the closet. Their wrists and ankles were tied, and their mouths were taped shut with adhesive tape.

Michael didn't recognize either one of them. The man's face was thin and pale, his hair short and brown. The woman's hair was dark and disheveled and her head was down, and...

My God! It was Ruth Carlson! My God, what was she doing here?

"Okay," the man with the droopy mustache said, putting his hand on Michael's back and pushing him into the closet. "Get down on your butt so I can get your legs tied up."

With his arms bound behind him, it was hard for Michael to sit down. He managed to do so by dropping to one knee, then the other, and then dropping to his side and pushing himself up to a sitting position with one elbow.

Ruth had raised her head and was staring at him, her eyes wide and frightened. She looked as though someone had beaten her up. Her face was bruised and swollen, and her blouse was ripped all the way down the front of it, exposing her slip.

The man sitting next to her was staring at Michael with a dazed look on his face. His nose was bloody, and the light sport shirt he was wearing was stained with blood.

With quick, deft movements, the man with the droopy mustache bound Michael's ankles together with the electric tape and plastic cord. Then he taped Michael's mouth shut with the adhesive tape.

"That'll keep you," he grunted.

Albert Crane stepped up to the doorway. "Bring Conklin out," he said to the man with the droopy mustache. "We're not through with him yet."

The man nodded, and, stepping around Michael, grabbed the arm of the man seated next to Ruth, and jerked him to his feet.

Come on, Conklin," he said. "They want to talk to you again."

The two of them brushed by Michael, the man with the droopy mustache half dragging Conklin out of the closet.

"Okay," Michael heard Albert Crane say. "Pull that tape off his mouth. I think he's ready to cooperate now."

Michael heard what sounded like adhesive tape being ripped, away from skin. Then he heard a husky, fearful voice that must have been Conklin's.

"Please," he heard the man say. "I've told you everything. Everything I know. You've got to believe me."

Michael heard the black-bearded thug laugh. "Don't worry, little man. We're not going to hurt you if you tell us the truth."

"I'm asking you once again," Michael heard Albert Crane say in a hard voice. "Tell us who the others are. The ones who've infiltrated our group here in Los Angeles."

"I told you." It was the husky voice of Conklin again. "I told you all I..."

"Listen, you stupid pig," Michael heard the black-bearded thug exclaim. "Who the hell d'you think you're talking to? You're not dealing with those imbecilic college kids now."

"Guess we'll have to beat it out of him," Albert Crane said in a cold voice. "Who wants to be first?"

"Please don't," Michael heard Conklin gasp in a pleading voice.

Michael heard a dull thud, and then the sound of someone choking in pain.

"Oh...oh...Please...please don't." It was Conklin. He was gasping. "Please..."

Michael heard another dull thud, and then another, and then still another. He glanced at Ruth. She had turned her face to the wall and was sobbing through the adhesive tape covering her mouth.

"Okay," he heard Crane say. "That's enough. Let him go. I think he wants to talk now."

"I don't think so," Michael heard the red-haired thug say. "I think he passed out."

Michael heard a heavy thump, as though someone had fallen to the floor.

"Do you think he's okay?" he heard the man with the droopy mustache ask. "He looks pretty bad to me."

"Yeah, he's okay," the black-bearded thug said. "See. He's moving his leg."

"Okay," Michael heard Albert Crane say. "Pick him up and put him back in the closet."

A moment later, the man with the droopy mustache came back into the closet carrying Conklin over his shoulder. Without any display of emotion, he dumped Conklin on the floor in front of Michael.

"Want me to tape his mouth shut again?" he shouted back over his shoulder to Albert Crane.

"What do you think, Ronald?" Crane said.

"I don't know," Michael heard Ronald Putnam say. "He doesn't seem to be breathing too well."

"Leave it on," Crane said, "so they have to keep looking at what we do to idiots who don't cooperate with us. All those cuts, and bruises and blood should help remind them,"

The man with the droopy mustache stood up. "Want me to stay up here and keep an eye on them?

Crane shook his head. "No, I don't think so. They're not going anywhere." He shrugged. "You might as well come downstairs and play some poker with us. We can check up on them later on."

Chapter 28

Michael glanced around the closet. They were going to have to get loose somehow, get out of there. No telling what those bastards had planned for them, were going to do to them. One thing he did know, though—they were crazy enough to kill all three of them.

He looked around the closet again. If only he had something sharp to cut through the electric tape and plastic cord binding his wrists and ankles.

Suddenly, he noticed the brass lip on the doorframe where the door latched when it was closed. Would that be sharp enough to cut through the tape and cord?

He started moving awkwardly backwards in a sitting position toward the doorframe. Ruth looked at him as though she thought he'd lost his mind. He maneuvered around the man named Conklin, who was still lying there unconscious.

The problem now was to get to his feet so he could back up against the brass lip, which stuck out about half an inch from the brass plate. He twisted and turned until he got to his knees, then leaned against the wall with one shoulder and worked himself up to a standing position.

With his back against the doorframe, he began to rub the tape and cord binding his wrists back and forth against the sharp edge of the brass lip. He couldn't see what he was doing, but for the next few minutes he stood there trying to cut through the tape and the cord.

Finally he gave up. He was hot and sweating and his back ached, and his wrists were sore and sticky with blood. He sighed and slid down against the doorframe to a sitting position on the floor. He was disappointed, frustrated, discouraged.

He saw Ruth staring at him, her face gray and pinched with anxiety. He wondered what she was thinking, wondered how she'd ever got herself mixed up in this God-awful mess, wondered who the devil the man Conklin was. If only he could talk to her!

My God, why hadn't he thought of it before? Why not use that brass lip on the doorframe to scrape the adhesive tape off his mouth?

Once again, he managed to get to his knees. Then, facing the brass lip, he tried to catch either end of the adhesive tape against the sharp edge of it. He tried a number of times without succeeding. All he was doing was irritating the skin around his mouth, and making it as sore as his wrists.

He rested a minute, then tried again. Suddenly one end of the adhesive tape caught against the brass lip and peeled back a bit. In only a few seconds, he managed to scrape the adhesive tape all the way off that cheek, and then all the way off his mouth. As he watched the adhesive tape fall to the floor, he felt a moment of elation. He'd done it, by God!

Instead of resting, he started making his way back toward Ruth. With great care, he maneuvered around the man named Conklin, who still lay there in that same position.

"Here," he said to Ruth, as he drew close to her. "Let me get that adhesive tape off your mouth. She frowned, looked puzzled.

"I'll use my teeth," he explained.

She hesitated, then nodded, and turned one side of her face toward him. He put his face up to hers and tried to catch the end of the adhesive tape on that cheek between his teeth. After several tries, he succeeded in doing so. With the adhesive tape firmly in his teeth, he pulled hard and the entire strip peeled back from her mouth, and he let it drop to the floor.

"Oh, Mike!" she burst out at once, sobbing. "What've I gotten us into?"

He tried to speak calmly. "We've got to get out of here as fast as we can." he said. "I think they're going to kill us."

She turned and looked at Conklin, her eyes filling with tears.

"Is he all right?"

"I don't know, Ruth." He paused. "Did you know they've got Carlene Edwards here, too?"

She winced. "Yes, I know."

"Well, we'd better not waste time. I'd better try to get you loose."

"How...how will you do that?"

"I'll use my teeth...try to chew through the cord and tape. If I can get your hands loose, then you can untie mine. And then we can get these things off our ankles. Can you get down on your side?"

"I...I think so."

"It'll be easier for me if you can."

"All right." She turned her shoulders and upper body to her right and then dropped awkwardly to her side.

"Oh, damn!" she cried. "My knee."

"What's wrong, Ruth?" He could see she was experiencing a lot of pain.

"I fell on the stairs when they brought me up here. I think I tore something in my knee."

Her knee did look bad. Through her torn stocking, it looked bruised and swollen, and the kneecap seemed to be twisted off to one side.

"Try to be careful," he cautioned her. "Try not to move it."

He dropped down on his side behind her. Her wrists were bound the same way his were—first with electric tape, and then with several loops of plastic cord. He tried biting into the plastic cord and was surprised he could. In less than a minute he's chewed all the way through it.

He began to get excited. So far, so good.

"Now I'll work on the electric tape," he said.

"Please hurry," she pleaded.

Getting the electrical tape off was even easier. After several tries, he caught one end of it between his teeth, then jerked on it until the entire strip came off her wrists. Now her hands were free.

"That does it," he said. "Now you can get this stuff off me."

Working himself back up to a sitting position, he watched sympathetically as Ruth, grimacing with pain, pushed herself on up to a sitting position beside him.

"Okay, Mike," she panted, turning to him. "Let's see your wrists."

He moved around until his back was to her.

"Oh, Mike," she cried. "Your poor wrists are bleeding."

"They're all right, Ruth. Go ahead. Untie them."

The knots were tight and hard to undo, but she kept struggling with them until they finally came loose. Then she stripped the electric tape off his wrists, and his hands were free, too.

He shook his hands and arms to get the circulation back in them, and then he untied Ruth's ankles, and then his. Then he struggled to his feet, his legs tingling as the blood rushed back through them.

"Check Fred, will you, please, Mike?" Ruth was looking up at him, her eyes red and fearful.

He realized that she was referring to Conklin. So that was his name...Fred Conklin.

"All right," he said.

He stepped over and knelt down beside Conklin. Conklin was still unconscious, and his breathing seemed weak and labored.

As carefully as he could, Michael pulled the adhesive tape off Conklin's mouth, then removed the plastic cord and electric tape from his wrists and ankles. Then he took a wool jacket off one of the hangers above him, folded it, and put it under

Conklin's head. Then he pulled a woman's long wool coat off another hanger and covered Conklin with it.

He stepped back toward Ruth.

"How is he?" she asked, her voice trembling.

He shook his head, "Not too good, I'm afraid."

Suddenly Conklin groaned and made a long, peculiar gasping sound. Michael went back to him. Conklin's face was gray, his eyes vacant looking. Michael pulled the coat down and put his ear to Conklin's chest. No sound. He reached for his neck, felt for his carotid artery. Nothing.

Michael glanced back at Ruth. She was staring at him with an anxious look on her face.

"I'm afraid he's gone," he said, keeping his voice low.

She stared at him. She didn't seem to understand.

"I'm sorry," he said. "I think he just died."

She still stared at him, still didn't seem to understand. Then, suddenly, she dropped her head and began to sob.

He pulled the coat up over Conklin's face and went back to her and put his hand on her shoulder, wishing there were some way he could comfort her.

After a few moments she raised her head and wiped the tears from her eyes with the back of her hand.

"I knew he was hurt badly," she choked. "But I..."

"I don't think there was anything we could've done to help him," he said gently.

Her face reddened. "They're...they're bastards. They're going to pay for this."

"Don't worry," he said. "They won't get away with it." He glanced toward the doorway. "I'm sorry, Ruth, but I'd better get going. I'd better find a way to get out of here. There's no telling when they'll come back to check on us."

She started to look fearful again.

"I'll check the bedroom windows," he said. "See if it'd be possible to tie some sheets together and get down that way." He put his hand on her shoulder. "I'll be right back."

"Be careful, Mike," she choked.

He nodded. "I'll be right back."

He stepped around Conklin's body and walked out into the bedroom. They had left the lights on there, too. He crossed over to the drapes and drew one back a little way. Shafts of light from a few first and second floor windows cut through the darkness exposing the ground down below.

He didn't like what he saw. The entire length of the house back there was built close to the edge of a ravine and the ravine looked deep and steep.

He shook his head, disappointed. There was no way he could get down that way—not even if he tied sheets and blanket together and slid down them. It would still be too far to drop, and even if he did drop, it was quite possible that he'd end up at the bottom of the ravine with more than a few broken bones.

He released the drape and went over to the door to the hallway, half expecting to find that Albert Crane had locked it. But when he turned the doorknob and pushed on it he was surprised to find he could open it.

He pushed the door open a few inches and peered out. The hallway was empty. His heart quickening with fear, he stepped on out and went quickly to the top of the stairs and peered down into the entrance hall. It was brightly lit, and it looked as though the rooms adjoining it were brightly lit, too.

He could hear the voices of several men coming from down below, and could smell cigar and cigarette smoke drifting up toward him. It was almost impossible to understand what the men were saying, but from the few words he could make out, he could tell they were playing poker.

He could see now that it would be far too dangerous to try to slip down the stairs and out the front door while they were down there. And the sad fact was, there was no telling how long they would be there. For all he knew, they might be there all night.

He turned away, his stomach knotting with discouragement, and hurried back down the hallway to the bedroom. He felt tired and dejected. There didn't seem to be any way out. And it was pointless to try to deceive himself about what that meant. Those bastards sure as hell weren't going to let Ruth and him go free.

Chapter 29

"What took you so long?" Ruth blurted. "I've been half out of my mind worrying about you."

"Sorry," Michael said. He shrugged. "I checked out the back of the house from the bedroom windows. And then I checked out the hallway and the stairway."

"The hallway and the stairway?" she said, frowning. "Wasn't that awfully dangerous?"

He shrugged again, deciding to be frank with her. "It's going to be harder to get out of here than I thought. The drop out the back windows is three stories down, and the back or the house is on the edge of a deep ravine. Even if I tied all the bedding together, we'd still have a long drop down and would probably end up with broken legs or a broken neck or back. So that rules that out."

"But what about the stairway? Is there any chance we could get out that way?"

"I'm not sure. The problem is, Crane and some of his henchmen are down there, just off the entrance hall, playing cards. So I guess that rules that out, too...unless we wait until everybody goes to bed or leaves, and that might be hours from now. Anyhow, they'll probably be coming back up here to check on us before they break up for the night. So I'm afraid our chances of getting out of here are very poor, if not impossible." He paused. "I'm sorry, Ruth. But that's the way it looks, the way it is. I don't want to mislead you or give you any false hopes."

She put her hand to her neck, her face turning somber. "So what are we going to do, Mike?" Her voice trembled a bit, "wait here and hope they don't play cards all night?"

"I guess that's about all we can do."

He dropped down beside her. If only they weren't on the third floor and that damned ravine wasn't down there. It only...Suddenly the idea struck him, and he mentally kicked himself for not having thought of it before.

He got quickly to his feet.

"What's wrong, Mike?" Ruth stared up at him, her forehead wrinkling with concern.

"I'm going to take another look out those windows. I think I might've missed something."

"Missed something?" She looked puzzled, doubtful.

"Yes. I'll explain when I get back. I shouldn't be gone more than a minute or two."

He went back out to the windows and once again drew one of the drapes to one side. The window had two sliding panels, each about three feet wide and three feet high. He slid one of the panels back a couple of feet. He couldn't see out very well because of the screen, so he pushed up on the knob that released the screen, and pushed it out and to one side, grasping the edge of it to keep it from falling. Then he stuck his head out and looked up.

The rain gutter was there, all right! And it looked as though it was within reaching distance. It was hard to tell in the darkness, though, how it was attached to the eave. If it was firmly attached, he could hang on to it and make his way, hand over hand, to either of the back corners of the house, where there should be a downspout he could slide down.

He stood there several seconds trying to make up his mind, then decided he didn't have any choice. Evidently it was the only way he could get out of this place. He'd better be damned sure, though, that the rain gutter would support his weight and that there was a downspout at the corner.

He slid the panel all the way back, then turned the already loosened screen at an angle and pulled it inside and leaned it up against the wall. Then he climbed up on the windowsill and gripped the side of the window frame with his left hand. Then, stretching up and out with his right hand, he reached for the rain gutter. He got a firm grip on it, and gave it a good, hard tug. Thank God! It was solid. It didn't budge one little bit. With luck, it should hold him.

Still gripping onto the window frame, he looked down toward the corner of the house near the garage. The downspout was visible in the bright light of the pole light there. It would be shorter to go that way, but much more dangerous. Anybody living in the quarters above the garage or anybody walking to or from the house would be able to see him.

He looked down toward the other corner, which was much farther away. It was dark down there, but he could make out a downspout. It would probably be much safer to go that way. At least he wouldn't have to worry about being seen by someone.

He climbed down off the windowsill and hurried back to the closet, wondering if what he was about to do was utter folly.

"Well," Ruth said, looking up at him with worried eyes, "what did you find out?"

"I think I can get out that way, after all." he said. He tried to look and sound confident.

She frowned. "But I thought you said it's too big a drop…that you could seriously hurt yourself if you tried it."

"I'm not going to go down that way, Ruth. I'm going to slide down a downspout."

"Downspout?"

"Yes. There's one on each corner of the back of the house."

She looked incredulous. "But can you do that...how will you get to it?"

"By the rain gutter. I can make my way hand over hand to it. It shouldn't be too hard. I'll slide down the one at the far corner. I don't think anyone will see me there."

She looked upset ."It sounds too dangerous, Mike. I don't think you should try it."

"I'm afraid there's no other way to get out of here, Ruth. If I can get down that way, I'll get to a phone and call the police, and they'll get you and Carlene Edwards out of here." He paused. "But I don't think it's safe to leave you here in the closet after I leave...in case they do came back to cheek on us."

She shrugged, "I can't go anywhere with my knee like this."

"I know, Ruth. But I noticed a closet in the hallway when they brought me down here, and I can hide you in there before I leave. Then I can take the bedding off the bed, tie it together, and hang it out the window. That way if they do come back to cheek on us, they'll think we both went out the window, and they won't go searching through the rest of the house for us, and you'll be safe that way."

She bit down on her lip. "It sounds awfully risky, Mike."

"I don't think we have any other choice, Ruth."

She hesitated.

"We'd better get started," he said. "I'm going to carry you, of course. Are you ready?"

She looked at Conklin's motionless body with tearful eyes, then looked back up at Michael.

"I'm ready," she said in a choked voice.

Chapter 30

He carried her out to the hallway, then down to the closet. He pushed the closet door all the way open with one foot and carried her in.

The closet was no more than four or five feet wide and about six feet deep. There were two upright vacuum cleaners in it, and several shelves along one wall with soaps, detergents, and cleaning compounds on them.

He put her down as gently as he could in back of the vacuum cleaners. There wasn't much space for her, but at least she could sit with her injured leg stretched out.

He bent and kissed her forehead. "Keep your courage up, Ruth. I'll come back as soon as I can."

She reached up, her eyes wide with apprehension, and gripped his wrist. "Be careful, Mike."

He nodded and stepped back to the door. "I'd better close this," he said, keeping his voice low.

"All right," she whispered.

He closed the door and started back down the hallway, afraid someone would step out of one or the doorways and see him, or that one of the thugs would suddenly appear and attack him. He wanted to run but forced himself to walk.

Once he was back inside the bedroom, he felt lightheaded from all the excitement. At least he wouldn't have to worry about Ruth now, he thought.

He hurried to the bed and pushed it over to the window he'd already opened and removed the screen from. Then he quickly stripped one blanket and the two sheets off the bed and tied them all together, making a makeshift rope of them. Then he tied one end to the leg of the bed nearest to the window, and slipped the other end out the window and let it slide on down the side of the house. Just as he feared, it fell far short of the ground. Thank God he'd decided not to go down that way, he thought. If he had, he might've killed or seriously injured himself.

His heart racing, he climbed up on the windowsill and crouched there, trying not to look down. Then steeling himself, he gripped one side of the window frame with his left hand and reached up for the rain gutter with his right. He grabbed it, took a deep breath, and swung out and away from the window.

For a scary moment he dangled there by one hand, his heart banging against his chest, then he reached out with his other hand, grabbed the rain gutter, and hung there by both hands.

He felt a brief moment of triumph. He'd done it! He was on his way! He was going to make it!

He started out, then, working his way, hand over hand, down toward the darkened far corner of the house. He couldn't have gone more than twenty feet when there was a sudden loud ripping sound.

Oh, God! The rain gutter was giving way!

Frantically he reached up and grabbed the edge of the tile roof with one hand, then reached up with his other hand and grabbed another part of the roof. Then, summoning up all his strength, he pulled himself up over the sagging section of gutter and onto the roof. He lay there then, gripping the tile and gasping for breath.

My God! He'd almost gone plunging down into that ravine. It would've been all over for him if he had. *And all over for Ruth and Carlene Edwards, too.*

He lay there a little longer, waiting for his heart to stop pounding against his chest. Then he crawled a little farther up the sloping roof and crouched there, peering around him. With a sinking feeling in his stomach, he realized there was no way he could get back into that bedroom now, even if he had to. In fact, it appeared that the only thing he could do now was make his way along the roof to the downspout he'd planned to slide down and see if he could still slide down it.

Thankful his shoes didn't have slick soles, he bent low and half crawled toward that corner of the house. When he got there, he bent down at once to see whether the downspout was firmly attached to the house. He gripped it and shook it hard, then swore to himself. It was hanging loose, probably held in place by only a few metal bands. It would never support him.

He crawled back from the corner of the roof, beginning to panic. What the devil was he going to do now? He realized there'd probably be downspouts on all four corners of the house, and that those out front might be attached firmly enough to support him. But he also realized that he'd be very conspicuous out there in all that light from the porch and that big water fountain.

But what else could he do? He couldn't think of anything—not a single thing! He'd just have to take the chance that he might be seen. And he'd better quit wasting time now and get going.

He crawled on up to the top of the roof, and then, exposed in the light from the porch and the water fountain, he started down the front side of the roof toward the corner that was farther away from the porch. Any second he expected to see someone walking up the sidewalk or driving up the driveway. But luck was with him. No one did.

When he reached that corner of the roof and tested the downspout there, he felt a keen sense of disappointment, even though he'd tried to prepare himself to be disappointed. The downspout was just like the one in back. It was just as loose, no doubt held in place the same way.

He swallowed hard, tried to keep calm, to think clearly. What in the devil should he do now? Should he check out the downspouts on the other side of the house, on the corners near the garage? Or would it be too dangerous? He'd really be exposed in all that light from the brightly lit pole lights over there, probably even more exposed than here in front. And there might be any number of people going back and forth between the house and the servants' quarters above the garage.

He shook his head, discouraged. Apparently there was only one sure way to get off the roof, and that was to jump off. But he wasn't stupid enough to do that. That would be absolute folly. Three stories were three stories. He'd probably break every bone in his body if he tried it, even kill himself.

What a rotten, lousy mess!

He turned and crawled back up to the top of the roof, and then crawled a few feet down the other side so he couldn't be seen by anyone out front. Then he leaned back on his elbows, wondering bleakly what he should do now.

Across the ravine, he could see the lights of several houses shining in the darkness. They looked quite near, as though he could reach out and touch them with his finger tips. But he knew they were actually a long way off, maybe even a mile or so.

Suddenly then, as if for the first time, he saw it. It wasn't very far from the room where they were holding Carlene Edwards captive. He'd been concentrating so hard on the rain gutter and the downspouts that he simply hadn't noticed it.

But there it was. A giant spruce or pine tree—it was too dark to tell which. It towered up from the ravine to a height five or ten feet above the edge of the roof, with its nearest branches no more than fifteen to twenty feet away.

His chest tightened with excitement. It just might be possible. It would be one hell of a jump, but by running down the roof to gain speed and momentum, he could throw himself out toward those branches, and with any luck at all, land safely in the bigger branches somewhere below them. And then he could make his way on down the tree to the bottom of the ravine.

Trying hard to keep calm, he crawled down to the edge of the roof directly across from the tree. From that vantage point, he could see that he'd underestimated the distance of the branches from the edge of the roof. They were at least twenty to thirty feet away. His stomach twisted with disappointment. He could never jump that far. Never...But wait! The branches down below—down where the trunk of the tree was rooted in the ravine—the branches there were much bigger, much thicker, and furthermore, they looked strong enough to catch and support him.

He began to get excited again. If he got off a good run down the sloping roof and leapt out as far as he could, he should land in those big branches farther down the tree.

He stared down at the branches for several long moments, then, taking a deep breath, he turned and started back up the roof, his heart beating hard and fast.

Chapter 31

Michael peered down the sloping roof to the tree. He'd given himself about thirty feet of running space. He prayed now that it would be enough.

Clenching his fists, he started to run, hoping fervently no one in the rooms below would hear him, and that he wouldn't stumble and fall, and that he wouldn't misjudge the edge of the roof.

Moments later, he was hurtling through the air. And then he was plunging downward. For a terrifying second he thought he would miss the tree. And then he crashed down into heavy layers of branches and grabbed one to hold onto.

He clung there, breathing hard, his hands stinging from the sharp needles and rough bark. In the light from the windows of the house, he saw he was about ten feet from the bottom of the ravine. He waited for his breathing to steady and his heart to slow down. Then, loosening his grip on the branch, he slid down toward the end of it. The branch bent under his weight, putting him closer to the ground.

He took a moment to prepare himself to drop, then let go. He landed heavily and fell forward on his hands and knees. As he struggled to his feet, he glanced up at the lighted windows of the house. Any moment, he expected to be caught in the glare of a flashlight or to hear the crack of gunfire.

Breathing hard, he turned and started for the opposite side of the ravine. Along the crest of it, he could see the lights of several homes. He felt a surge of elation. With any luck at all, he'd be calling the police in only a matter of minutes.

The bottom of the ravine was strewn with rocks and scrubs, and it was slow and tough going. But finally, sweating heavily, he got to the other side and started up the steep and rugged bank in front of him.

By the time he got to the top, he was gasping for breath. He knelt on one knee and rested, trying to orient himself. Not more than an arm's length away was a chain-link fence that looked to be about eight feet high and ran all the way along the edge of the ridge. Behind it were several big and impressive-looking homes. Most of them had lights on. The nearest one was about seventy-five feet back from the fence. It was probably the best place to get help, he decided.

He got to his feet and somehow managed to clamber up and over the fence. As he dropped to the lawn below, the whole area around him suddenly burst into light and two large Doberman pinschers came hurtling toward him.

He panicked and whirled and tried to scramble back up the fence. There was a sudden explosion right behind him, and someone shouted, "Hold it right there!"

Michael stiffened and dropped back down. A man stood next to an oval-shaped swimming pool, pointing a shotgun at him.

"Stay!" the man ordered the growling dogs crouched next to him. "Stay right here." Then he spoke to Michael. "Face the fence, and put both hands above your head, or I'll blow you into pieces."

Michael raised his hands above his head and faced the fence.

"Now," the man said, "keep your hands above your head and turn around, slow and easy."

Michael turned around, trying to ignore the growling, menacing Doberman pinschers.

"Look," he blurted. "I wasn't trying to break in. I've got to call the police. The Rose Queen's a prisoner in a house over there." He nodded back over his shoulder toward the houses on the ridge across the ravine. "I just escaped from there."

The man, who was stocky and white-haired, started to say something, then stopped.

Michael could see he didn't believe him. "Please," he said. "Let me call Lieutenant Ferraro of the Pasadena police. He can vouch for me. I'm an attorney here in Pasadena. My name's Michael Donovan. I..." He started to reach for his billfold to show the man his driver's license and business card.

"Hold it!" the man said. "Keep both hands up where I can see them."

"Look," Michael said. "I—"

"Save it for the police!" the man interrupted in a hard, no-nonsense voice. "My wife has already called them."

Although it seemed much longer to Michael, the police arrived a few minutes later. The man's worried-looking wife brought them out to where her husband and Michael were still standing. There were two of them, both in uniform. One was tall and swarthy, the other, short and fair.

Michael showed the officers his driver's license and business card, and the card Lt. Ferraro had given him.

"Several men are holding the Rose Queen and my partner's wife prisoner in one of those big homes across the ravine back there," he said, trying to speak calmly. "I think they're planning to kill them. You'd better call Lieutenant Ferraro and let him know. It's urgent to act right away."

"Use our phone if you like," volunteered the white-haired man with the shotgun. He no longer sounded hard and skeptical.

The tall, swarthy officer nodded. "It'll be easier than calling from our car, and Lieutenant Ferraro will probably want to talk to Mr. Donovan here."

The phone was in a large family room just off the patio. The tall, swarthy officer phoned Lt. Ferraro at his home, and the lieutenant answered at once.

"This is Sergeant Kevin Sheldon," the officer said. "Sorry to disturb you at home, Lieutenant, but we answered a call about a break-in up here in the hills northwest of the Rose Bowl. The man who did it says his name is Michael Donovan and that he's an attorney and that he knows you. He says he was kidnapped by the people who kidnapped the Rose Queen and that he just escaped from them. He says they're holding her in a house not far from here."

The sergeant stopped talking and didn't say anything for few seconds, evidently listening to what Lt. Ferraro had to say. Then the sergeant said, "Yes sir, Lieutenant, it's him, all right. We checked his driver's license and business card, and he showed us a card he says you gave him. He says they're not only holding the Rose Queen prisoner, but they've also got his partner's wife there, and the body of some man they just killed."

The sergeant paused, then said, "Yes sir, Lieutenant," and he turned and handed the receiver to Michael. "The lieutenant wants to speak to you," he said.

Before Michael could say anything, the lieutenant said, "I'll be brief, Mr. Donovan. Is the girl okay?"

"I think so," Michael said. "But it's hard to tell. She's heavily sedated."

"Sergeant Sheldon said they're holding your partner's wife there, too, and that they killed some man they were holding prisoner with her."

"That's right. I was there when it happened."

"What about your partner's wife? Is she okay?"

"Yes, she is...except for a badly injured knee."

"How many people are involved...are holding them?"

"I'm not sure. Five men that I know of. Plus a woman. There might be more. And probably are."

The lieutenant paused. "Better let me speak to Sergeant Sheldon again," he said.

For the next two minutes or so, Sgt. Sheldon listened intently to the lieutenant without speaking. Then finally, he said, "Okay, Lieutenant," and handed the receiver to the stocky, white-haired man. "Lieutenant Ferraro wants to speak to you," he said.

The man took the receiver. "This is Harold Webster," he said. He was silent a few seconds, then said, "Our address is 1475 North Mirimar Drive." He was silent once again, then he said, "The house is on a ridge directly across from us, and the street over there is North Valente Road." He paused. "Yes, I will," he said, and handed the receiver back to Sgt. Sheldon.

The conversation between Sgt. Sheldon and Lt. Ferraro lasted three or four minutes, with Sgt. Sheldon once again listening intently, and saying only "yes" or "no" to whatever Lt. Ferraro was saying.

After Sgt. Sheldon hung up, he turned and faced them. "Lieutenant Ferraro and the Special Enforcement Team will meet us a block or so down the street from the house where they're holding the girl," he said. "He wants us to leave right away and get there first, and to stay out of sight until he and the Enforcement Team get there. He wants you to come with us, Mr. Donovan, so you can tell us the layout of the house and answer any questions that might come up."

Chapter 32

Michael saw the two giant palm trees with the wooden bench between them loom up in the darkness in front of them.

"That must be Valente Road," he said, leaning forward from the backseat. "I recognize those two palm trees with the bench between them. There on the corner."

Sgt. Sheldon was driving, and the short, fair-faced officer, Cpl. Franklin, was sitting next to him.

"I'll check the street sign," the sergeant said, slowing down.

Michael was right. It was Valente Road...North Valente Road.

"It's not too far from here," Michael said. "Only a mile or so up the hill."

Sgt. Sheldon glanced back over his shoulder at him. "Point out the house as soon as you can. We don't want to get too close to it."

Michael nodded. "I will."

They drove in silence up the dark, winding street to the top of the hill, then moved slowly along its ridge. Michael recognized the big homes they were passing now, the ones behind the big walls and the ornamental iron gates.

"Better slow down," he said to Sgt. Sheldon. "The house is just a few houses up from here. On the right side."

The sergeant nodded and slowed down. They were barely moving now.

"There," said Michael, pointing up ahead. "It's that big three-story house up there. The pink-colored one. You can see the red tile roof from here."

The sergeant pulled over to the curb and turned off the headlights. "We'll wait here for the lieutenant," he said. "It'll give him and the others plenty of space to park behind us."

In less than ten minutes, an unmarked car drew up and parked behind them. A man climbed out and hurried toward them.

"It's him," Cpl. Franklin said.

Sgt. Sheldon rolled down his window, and Lt. Ferraro stepped up beside it. His face looked gaunt in the darkness.

"Which house is it?" he asked.

The sergeant pointed it out to him. "That big pink house up there to our right," he said.

The lieutenant stood there studying it for a few moments. Then he leaned back down and said. "Let's slip up there and get a better look at it before the Special Enforcement Team gets here." He hesitated. "You'd better stay here, Corporal. In case the others get here before we get back."

The corporal looked disappointed. "Yes, sir," he said.

"What about me?" Michael said. "Want me to come, too?"

The lieutenant nodded. "You can tell us what you know about the inside layout or the house and anything else you think might be important.

Staying out of sight behind a row of tall shrubs on their side of the street, Lt. Ferraro, Sgt. Sheldon, and Michael slipped past several big homes and on up to the front of the big pale-pink house.

The lieutenant indicated the lighted house number 2212 on one of the columns of the front porch.

"Help me remember that number, Sergeant," he said in a low voice. "We may need it a little later.

They spent the next minute or two carefully surveying the external layout of the house and the garage, and the grounds around them. Then the lieutenant asked Michael to give him a brief description of the interior of the house and its layout.

When Michael finished, the lieutenant said. "About that big ravine in back you mentioned—is there any way to get inside the house from back there?"

Michael shook his head. "I don't know. But I don't think so."

Sgt. Sheldon spoke up. "I see a side door, though. It's probably used to go back and forth between the house and the garage."

"I suppose there are servants' quarters above the garage," Michael said. "See the stairway there?"

Sgt. Sheldon nodded. "Looks that way. They might even have some of those White Unity characters living up there."

"They might," Lt. Ferraro said. He looked back toward the house. "Apparently the front and side doors are the only way we can get inside the house...unless, of course, we go through those first-floor windows." He turned to Michael. "You said both the girl and your friend are on the third floor, didn't you?"

"Yes, that's right," Michael said. "But they're in different places. The girl's in a bedroom down at one end of the hallway. And Mrs. Carlson's actually hiding in a closet near the middle of the hallway. I tied some bedding together in the bedroom where they were holding us to make it look as though Mrs. Carlson had escaped out the window with me."

A few moments later they returned to the car, and Lt. Ferraro got into the backseat next to Michael.

"What I'd like you to do now," the lieutenant said, taking a small notebook and a ballpoint pen out of the inside pocket of his jacket and handing them to Michael. "What I'd like you to do is draw a rough diagram of the interior of the house for the Special Enforcement Team." He took a pen-sized flashlight out of the other inside pocket and turned it on holding it at an angle so that Michael would have enough light to make out the diagram. "Before you get started on the interior," he added, "you'd better draw an outline of the exterior of the house, showing where the front and side doors are, and indicating that there's a deep ravine in back and that there's probably no way to get in the house from back there."

Michael quickly did so, trying to make the outline as simple and clear as he could.

"Now, show the interior of the house and where the girl and your friend are on the third floor."

Michael drew a plan of the third floor, showing Carlene Edwards in a bedroom down at the end of the hallway to the left of the stairs, and Ruth in a hallway closet a short distance to the right of the stairs.

"Now," said Lt. Ferraro, "where's the body of the man they killed? You'd better show where it is, too."

"It's on the third floor, too," Michael said, "in the closet of a bedroom to the right of the stairs and at the end of the hall." He showed with an X where the bedroom and closet were. "It's where they kept the three of us before they killed the man, and before Mrs. Carlson and I got loose."

"Better indicate where the stairs to the upper floors are relative to the front door," the lieutenant said.

Michael used several arrows to show that the stairs were to the right of the entrance hall, and that they went straight up to the second and third floors.

The lieutenant paused. "Can you think of anything else we should show about the layout of the house...and the third floor in particular?"

"No, I don't think so," Michael said.

"Can you think of anything we should know about the people in there?"

Michael shook his head. "Not really. As I told you on the phone, I know there are five men and one woman there. But there may be more, and probably are. You already know that they're fanatics and very dangerous, and that they're willing to kill."

"Sorry to interrupt," said Sgt. Sheldon. "But the Special Enforcement Team is pulling in behind us now."

The lieutenant peered out the back window, then turned to Michael and took the notebook and pen back from him.

"Hold tight right here. Mr. Donovan. I'll take Sergeant Sheldon and Corporal Franklin with me and go back and brief the Enforcement Team. Then I'm going to have the sergeant and the corporal stay with them and help them any way they can. I should be back in a couple of minutes or so, and then I'm going to depend on you to help me with something I've got planned."

Lt. Ferraro and the two officers got out and hurried back down the street past the lieutenant's car. In the darkness, Michael could see a number of vehicles parked along the curb down from them. He made out a van, an ambulance, and several police cars. He saw several men get out and gather around Lt. Ferraro and the two officers. Seconds later, he saw the slender beam of a flashlight moving back and forth inside the circle of men. He guessed they were looking at the diagrams he'd drawn for them.

He turned back and looked apprehensively toward the pink-colored house, wondering whether Crane and the others had discovered he'd escaped yet. As he sat there, he saw Lt. Ferraro come hurrying back toward the car with two men wearing dark clothes. One of the men went past the car and on up the street. Lt. Ferraro and the other man stopped on Michael's side of the car. The man with the lieutenant was carrying a portable telephone. Lt. Ferraro opened the door and asked Michael to step out.

"This is Sergeant Clay," he said, "and this is Mr. Donovan."

Michael and the sergeant nodded to each other.

"The officer who just went up the street," the lieutenant explained to Michael, "will serve as a lookout and a go-between for us. Sergeant Clay here will set up his portable three-way phone in that house there"—he indicated the impressive-looking two-story stucco house at the end of the driveway—"if the people who live there are willing to cooperate with us." He paused. "If we can't set it up there, we'll try that place across the street." He pointed at a rambling brick house across from them with lights showing in most of its windows. Then he turned and waved to the cluster of men still standing down near the van. Several of them started moving up the street toward them, and those who remained started moving back toward the vehicles along the curb.

"Okay," Lt. Ferraro said, turning back to Michael and Sgt. Clay. "Let's go."

The three of them hurried up the driveway to the big stucco house, which looked pale blue in the light from its windows.

Lt. Ferraro rang the doorbell, and, moments later, the porch light came on, and the door opened a few inches.

"What do you want?" a gray-haired man asked from behind a security chain. He looked and sounded unfriendly.

Lt. Ferraro pulled out his billfold and showed the man his badge.

"I'm Lieutenant Ferraro of the Pasadena Police Department," he said. "And this officer with me is Sergeant Clay." He indicated Michael with a slight nod of his head. "This gentleman is Michael Donovan, an attorney." He put his billfold back in his pocket. "We're here," he said, "because we've learned that the Pasadena Rose Queen and a woman friend of Mr. Donovan's are being held prisoner in a house just up the street, a large pink one. With your permission, we'd like to set up our portable phone inside your house and contact the kidnappers. We won't tell them where we're calling from, of course, and you'll be perfectly safe." He paused. "I know it's an inconvenience, but will you help us?"

The man hesitated, his eyes narrowing behind his gold-rimmed glasses.

"All right," he said after a moment. "My wife's health isn't very good, but I guess it won't upset her too much." He looked in the direction of the pink house up the street. "I haven't the slightest idea who's living in that place now," he added. "The former owner, a man by the name of John Whittier, died a little over a year ago, and I understand someone's been renting the house ever since then. But do come in. We'll help in any way we can."

Chapter 33

THEY STEPPED INSIDE AND THE MAN closed the door behind them. He was wearing a tan terrycloth bathrobe and brown slippers.

"I'm afraid I didn't give you my name," he said with an apologetic little shrug. "I'm Carl MacDonald." He glanced at the portable telephone the sergeant was carrying. "Where do you want to use that, Sergeant?"

"Anywhere we can plug it in," Sergeant Clay said. "But the closer to the front door, the better."

"We've got a lookout up there by the house." Lt. Ferraro explained. "We want to be able to contact him as fast as possible, if it becomes necessary to do so."

"How about the living room over there?" Mr. MacDonald said. "Or you can use the library across the hall. You're welcome to use either one."

"Either's fine," the sergeant said.

A frail-looking white-haired woman in a blue dressing gown appeared at the top of the stairs.

"Who is it, Carl?" she called out.

"No need to be alarmed, Grace. It's the police. They've asked for some help, is all."

Her voice sharpened. "Police?" She reached out for the

handrail for support. "What do the police want?"

"There's nothing to be upset about, dear. Apparently those people living in the Whittier place are the ones that kidnapped the Rose Queen. They're holding her and another woman captive up there, in fact."

The woman's eyes widened. "The Rose Queen?...Just up the street?" she said, her voice trembling.

"Yes, dear. I'm afraid so."

The woman's stunned look turned fearful. "Will there be any shooting?"

"Now, Grace. You don't have to worry about that. These men know what they're doing. They're simply going to set up a portable telephone here and call up there and talk to the kidnappers. They won't let them know they're calling from here, of course."

The woman, still looking fearful, started down the stairs.

"I'm going to make myself some tea," she said in a quavery voice. "I'll be in the kitchen if you want me."

"If you don't mind," Lt. Ferraro said to Mr. MacDonald, "while the sergeant's getting the portable telephone set up, I'd like to use a phone of yours to call the telephone company."

"There's one in the library," Mr. MacDonald said. "You might as well make your call in there, and while you're doing that, the sergeant can set up your portable telephone in there, too."

"Good idea," said the lieutenant.

The library was a comfortable-looking room with a large mahogany desk, leather furniture, and rows of books in built-in bookcases along two walls. While Sgt. Clay set up the portable telephone and headsets in the nearest corner, Lt. Ferraro used the phone on the desk to make his call to the telephone company.

Michael and Mr. MacDonald stood in the doorway watching them. It was quite evident to Michael that the police department had special arrangements with the telephone company for emergencies like this. Within seconds, Lt. Ferraro had the telephone number for 2212 North Valente Road.

As soon as he hung up, Sgt. Clay handed headsets to him and Michael.

"Before we start," Lt. Ferraro said, "let me explain to Mr. Donovan what to expect." He turned to Michael. "Sergeant Clay will ask to speak to this Albert Crane, since you think he's the one in charge. The sergeant will tell him that you and Mrs. Carlson have escaped, and that our Special Enforcement Team has surrounded the house. I may ask you to speak to Crane so he'll know you got away and can identify him and all the rest of them."

He paused. "Any questions?"

Michael shook his head. "No, I don't think so."

"Okay," the lieutenant said. "Then let's put these headsets on and get started."

The sergeant bent over the telephone and tapped in the number Lt. Ferraro had given him, and a woman answered immediately.

"Hello," she said. "This is Claudia Crane speaking."

Michael recognized her voice at once. It was Albert Crane's wife. He got a quick mental picture of her: brown hair, thin face, sharp dark eyes.

"I'd like to speak to Dr. Crane," the sergeant said.

"May I ask who's calling?" Mrs. Crane's voice was pleasant, cordial.

"He doesn't know me, but it's very important that I speak to him," the sergeant said.

She didn't say anything for a moment. Then she said, "Just a moment, please. I'll call him."

Seconds later, Albert Crane's clear, self-assured voice rose in Michael's earpiece.

"Dr. Crane speaking," he said. "Who is this? What's this all about?"

"I'm a police officer with the Pasadena Police Department," the sergeant said. "We know that you're holding the Rose Queen, Carlene Edwards, prisoner, and we demand that you release her immediately. Our Special Enforcement Team has surrounded your house and is prepared to rescue her by force if necessary."

"Is this some kind of joke?" Albert Crane exclaimed. "If it is, it's not at all funny."

"It's no joke," said the sergeant, his voice still calm and measured. "Bring Miss Edwards out through the front door and turn her over to us. Do this yourself. When she's safely in our hands, the others can come out, one at a time. We understand you may have people in the quarters over the garage. Call them and tell them to stay where they are until we tell them they can come out. Now, there are—"

"Just a minute!" Crane cut in. His voice was trembling with anger. "I let you ramble on as long as I did because I thought you were playing some kind of silly joke on me. But I realize now that's not the case. I don't know where you got this asinine story, but I—"

"Hold on!" Lt. Ferraro broke in. "This is Lieutenant Ferraro, and I'm in charge here. There's no way you can bluff your way out of this. Mr. Donovan escaped only a short time ago, and he's right here with me. If it's proof you want that it's all over for you, here he is."

Lt. Ferraro turned to Michael, waiting for him to speak. Michael's throat tightened. "This is Michael Donovan," he said. "You'd better do exactly what the lieutenant and the sergeant told you to do. There's no sense in getting yourself hurt...or any of the others. You're an intelligent man. Do what they've told you to do."

Lt. Ferraro held up his hand, signaling to Michael that he wanted to speak to Albert Crane again.

"This is Lieutenant Ferraro again," he said. "As Mr. Donovan said, there's no sense in you and the others getting hurt. We've got the entire house surrounded with sharpshooters. And we've got enough tear gas to fill all three floors. So let's not waste any more time. Bring the Rose Queen out, and then everybody else can come out. We'll give you just ten minutes to do so. If you haven't complied by then, we're coming in after you."

Albert Crane didn't reply for a few moments. Michael thought he might've left the phone. Then, suddenly, he spoke up.

"All right," he said. He sounded conciliatory. "We'll cooperate with you. Give me a minute or two to tell the others what you want done, and to contact those in the garage and give them your message. And then I'll get the girl ready—she's heavily sedated—and bring her out."

Lt. Ferraro flashed Sgt. Clay and Michael a victorious smile, then turned his attention back to Albert Crane.

"Don't try any tricks," he warned him, "or you'll dearly regret it." He glanced at his watch. "Remember, you've got no more than ten minutes. That's the absolute limit."

"All right," Crane said. "I'll bring the girl out in half that time."

Lt. Ferraro took off his headset and motioned to Sgt. Clay and Michael to do so, too.

"So far, so good," the lieutenant said. He turned to Mr. MacDonald, who had been standing in the doorway watching them all through their exchanges with the two Cranes. "Is it all right if the sergeant leaves this phone equipment here for a little while?" the lieutenant asked. "We're going to need his help up the street."

"Yes, of course, it is," Mr. MacDonald said. "Leave it for as long as you like."

The lieutenant turned to Michael. "I'm going to have to ask you to stay here till we get back. We never know what kind of trouble we'll run into in a hostage situation like this." He looked at Mr. MacDonald again. "Is it all right with you if Mr. Donovan stays here till we roust all those characters out? In a situation like this only professionals should be involved."

"He's welcome to stay." Mr. MacDonald said. He looked at Michael. "Perhaps you'd like a cup of coffee while—"

"Wait a sec!" cried the sergeant with a startled look. "Did you hear that?"

"Hear what?" said the lieutenant.

"Gunfire!" cried the sergeant, almost choking on the word. He pointed in the direction of the pink house up the street. "It's coming from up there!"

Chapter 34

As Lt. Ferraro and Sgt. Clay rushed out of the house, the crackle of gunfire grew louder, more intense.

Michael swung toward Mr. MacDonald. "I can't stay here," he blurted. "I've got to get up there. A close friend of mine is in that house."

Before Mr. MacDonald could reply, Michael was dashing out the front door. He saw Lt. Ferraro and Sgt. Clay running up the street, and he started after them.

Up ahead, several police cars were parked along the curb with their spotlights trained on the big pink house. A number of officers were crouched behind the cars, firing toward the house. An officer in body armor stood behind a tree up near the water fountain, lobbing tear gas into the windows of the house.

Michael winced. My God, a small war was underway!

He watched as Lt. Ferraro and Sgt. Clay ran to one of the cars parked farther up the street and joined the two officers crouched behind it. He waited a moment, then ran to the nearest car and ducked behind it, praying that Ruth and Carlene Edwards were all right. With his heart thudding against his chest, he peered over the trunk of the car toward the house. In the glare of the spotlights, he saw two men lying on the sidewalk out front. Only a few feet separated them. One was the thug with the black beard, the other was the man with the droopy mustache who had been guarding Ruth and her friend Conklin.

One of the spotlights shifted to the outside stairway of the garage. A man Michael had never seen before stood there, firing what looked like a sawed-off automatic rifle. Suddenly the man dropped the rifle and slumped against the railing. There was another burst of gunfire from one of the first-floor windows of the house.

Someone using a bullhorn up the street from Michael bellowed, "Okay, in there! In the house and in the garage. It's all over. Throw your guns out the door, and come out with your hands over your head. Do you hear? It's all over!"

Several seconds went by. No one came out of the house or out of the living quarters above the garage.

"I'm warning you," the man with the bullhorn bellowed. "Come out right now, or we're coming in after you."

Michael looked at the front door of the house and then at the side door, which faced the garage. No one was coming out of either door. He looked at the top of the outside stairway of the garage, where the man lay slumped against the railing. Two men with their hands over their head were stepping out of the door. He watched as they stepped around the body of the man slumped there and started down the stairway, one after the other. Michael had never seen either one of them before. They were starangers.

"You two men on the stairs there!" the man with the bullhorn yelled. "Come out to the street! And keep those hands up all the way!"

Michael looked back toward the house. No one was coming out of either the front or side door. Suddenly he saw the drapes in the big bay window on the first floor burst into flames. And then, seconds later, flames flared up in the windows of the rooms on each side of it.

One of the officers up the street—it sounded like Lt. Ferraro—shouted for someone to get on a car radio and ask for fire trucks and a transport van.

Michael glanced back at the house. Three women in street clothes had burst out of the front door, looking disheveled and wild-eyed. He recognized all three of them. The one in front was Claudia Crane. The other two he'd seen with Ruth Carlson at Benito's—the plump, sandy-haired woman with the masculine voice, and the thin, gray-haired woman. They all ran down across the lawn and huddled behind one of the police cars parked along the curb.

Sgt. Clay and another officer ran over and handcuffed the women and put them in the backseat of the car.

Suddenly someone darted out of the side door of the house and went zigzagging toward the garage, firing a handgun in the general direction of the police cars.

There was an answering barrage of gunfire from behind the police cars, and the man crumpled to the sidewalk not far from where Michael was. Michael saw who it was then. It was the red-haired thug.

Michael looked back toward the house. A large part of the first floor appeared to be in flames now. Four men ran out of the front door with their hands above their head. Michael recognized only one of them. Ronald Putnam. The bastard who'd tried to rape Ellen. He looked ready to collapse.

Michael saw Lt. Ferraro dash to the police car just up from him and crouch there, gun in hand. Michael ran up to him.

"Somebody's got to get Ruth Carlson and Carlene Edwards out of there," Michael shouted. "I'm going in, but I'll need some help."

The lieutenant grabbed Michael's arm, his eyes focusing on something over Michael's shoulder.

Michael swung around. Carlene Edwards stood in the front doorway. She was wearing the same blouse, skirt, and sweater she had worn the day she was kidnapped. Albert Crane stood there beside her, his arm around her waist, supporting her.

"Don't shoot!" Crane shouted at them. "We're bringing her out."

Lt. Ferraro turned toward the man with the bullhorn, who was two cars up from them.

"Tell everybody to hold their fire!" he yelled at him. "Hold your fire!" the man with the bullhorn bellowed. "Everybody hold your fire!"

Michael thought he saw Crane speak to Carlene. Then, with his arm still around her waist to support her, Crane started walking her across the porch and down the steps. She looked limp, ready to drop.

"How about some help?" Crane shouted. "She's still half unconscious."

Suddenly there was a sharp popping sound. And then another. Crane clutched his chest with his free hand, and for a second seemed to freeze there. Then his knees buckled, and he fell face down to the sidewalk. Carlene wavered there a moment, then pitched forward full length beside him.

Michael stared at them, stunned. Then out of the corner of his eye, he saw the black-bearded thug who was lying on the sidewalk hoist himself on one elbow. A wisp of smoke drifted upward from the handgun he was holding.

A shot suddenly rang out close to Michael, momentarily deafening him. Through a blur, he saw the black-bearded thug's head snap back, saw him pitch over on his side and lie still, his gun still clenched in his hand.

Chapter 35

An officer dashed up the sidewalk and dropped to his knees beside Carlene Edwards. Another officer ran over to the black-bearded thug, checked him, and then ran to the man with the droopy mustache who was lying nearby. Still another officer ran over to the red-haired thug sprawled out close to Michael's car.

Two fire trucks came roaring up, lights flashing, sirens wailing. Moments later, several firemen wearing backpacks and oxygen masks were plunging through the smoking front door of the house.

Michael saw a couple of white-coated ambulance attendants hurrying up to Carlene Edwards with a gurney, and he ran after them. When he got there, Carlene's eyes were closed and blood was oozing from her forehead.

"Is she all right?" he blurted.

"I think so," said the attendant who was examining her. "I think she just passed out, is all. She seems to be breathing okay. I think it's just a superficial wound on her head there."

"Thank God," Michael said.

The two attendants carefully lifted Carlene and placed her on the gurney and strapped her down. As they started down the sidewalk, Michael turned and looked toward the front door of the house for Ruth Carlson. There was still no sign of her. His stomach cramped with fear. He'd better go in and get her himself.

Suddenly he saw her. Two firemen burst out of the smoking doorway, carrying her between them. As they came hurrying down the steps of the porch, Michael rushed up to meet them.

"Ruth!" he cried.

She opened her eyes and saw him. "Oh, Mike," she choked. "You made it!" Her eyes filled with tears. "Be sure they get Fred. I told them he's in the closet."

"I will, Ruth."

"Sorry," one of the firemen said, "we've got to get her to the ambulance." They started moving on down the sidewalk.

"Tell Norm I'm all right," Ruth cried back over her shoulder to Michael. "Tell him not to worry about me."

Michael nodded. "I'll tell him," he promised.

He looked around for Lt. Ferraro and saw him standing down by the van. He hurried down to speak to him.

"Mrs. Carlson's worried about the man in the closet. She's afraid they'll leave his body there."

Lt. Ferraro's expression softened. "She needn't worry. I'll take care of it." He started looking around for a fellow officer.

"What hospital are they taking Mrs. Carlson and the girl to?" Michael asked.

"I think the Huntington." the lieutenant said.

Michael hesitated. "If it's all right with you, I'm going to get out of here. "I want to let my partner know his wife's all right."

Lt. Ferraro nodded. "Thanks for all you've done, Mr. Donovan. You've been a great help." He shook hands with Michael. "I'll get in touch with you sometime tomorrow and let you know what we've learned about all this."

It didn't surprise Michael that the black-bearded thug hadn't left his car key in the ignition. He didn't need it, though. He always carried an extra one in his billfold.

As he backed out of the driveway, he realized how stiff and sore and tired he was. It was hard to believe what he'd just gone through. Poor Ruth. He wondered how she figured into all this. It was obvious that she had been emotionally involved with that fellow Conklin. But how did all that come about? He shook his head and sighed. He felt awfully sorry for her.

But what about Norm? He'd be shocked when he learned Ruth had been kidnapped and was involved somehow in this crazy mess. He hated the thought of having to tell him.

As he expected, Norm was still up, waiting for Ruth to come home. When he saw Michael at the door, he was shocked, and when Michael recounted the events of the night, he looked sick to the stomach.

"You sure Ruth's all right?" he asked, his voice husky and fearful.

"Yes, Norm, I'm sure."

"And she's at the Huntington hospital, you say?" He glanced at his watch. "It's pretty late...after one, in fact. I wonder if I could get in to see her."

Michael shrugged. "Why don't you call and see?"

"I think I will."

It took Norm only a few seconds to make the call. When he hung up, he was frowning.

"No luck?" asked Michael.

Norm shook his head. "Afraid not. They want me to wait till morning. They said she's been given pain medication and a sedative and is already sound asleep." His eyes hardened and he clenched his fists. "Why the hell did they kidnap her, Mike? Why kidnap Ruth?"

"I don't know, Norm. I'm as confused as you are."

"Maybe it would never've happened if I'd gone with her."

"I don't understand. Gone where?"

Norm shrugged. "A teacher friend of hers...I'm quite sure you don't know her. This friend was having a post-game party. I just didn't feel like going, and I told Ruth to go on without me." He sighed. "You know, Mike, I thought the Cranes were oddballs right from the start. But I never would've dreamt they'd be involved in something as totally crazy as this." He dropped into the armchair across from Michael. "Conklin did seem to be a pretty nice guy, though. It's a damned shame, what they did to him."

"Who was he anyway? Ruth didn't say."

"He's the guy I told you about at the party last night, the Cal State prof who introduced her to the Cranes."

Michael was surprised. "So that's the guy."

Norm rubbed the back of his neck. "I don't know what to make of all this, Mike. It's all so unbelievable. Why in the world would the Cranes want to kidnap Ruth and Conklin? They're supposed to be good friends of theirs. And what in God's name were they trying to get out of Conklin by beating him up that way? And why would they, of all people, a medical doctor and a nurse...why would educated persons like that be involved in such heinous acts as that?"

"I don't know, Norm."

They talked a little while longer—Michael could see that Norm didn't want to be alone, that he needed someone to talk to—and then, finally, Michael said, "I'm pretty tired, Norm. And it's awfully late. So I'd better get going."

Norm nodded, looking a bit sheepish. "Forgive me for keeping you up like this, Mike—especially after what you've been through."

Norm walked out to the front porch with him. "Thanks for coming all the way up here to let me know about Ruth," he said. He gripped Michael's hand. "I do appreciate it, Mike."

Michael felt awfully sorry for him. He was such a good and decent man, and Ruth was the one and only love or his life.

"That's all right, Norm. I'm just sorry I had to bring you bad news."

They said good night and Michael walked on out to his car. He was still puzzled about how Ruth fit into all this mess. And it did seem rather clear to him that Norm probably didn't know as much about it as he did. Oh well, Lt. Ferraro would probably be able to make sense of all this and provide all the answers before this new day was over.

Chapter 36

The moment Michael walked in the office that morning, Dottie jumped up from her desk, her face flushing with emotion.

"Are you all right, Michael?" she cried.

"Why, yes, Dottie," he said. "I'm fine."

"Well, it's all over the news what happened last night!" She stepped around her desk and moved up close to him, inspecting his face the way his mother used to when he was a boy and she thought he wasn't feeling well. "You sure you're all right?"

"I'm fine, Dottie." He smiled and patted her shoulder. "Don't let these little scratches fool you. Anyhow, what're you doing here? Norm and I told you to take the day off. Don't you ever take our orders seriously?"

"Don't change the subject, Michael." She pushed her glasses back against the bridge of her nose, her eyes glinting. "Now tell me. What was that all about last night? I still can't believe you and Ruth were involved in something so...so incredible."

Michael shrugged and proceeded to give her enough information to satisfy her temporarily, then he asked whether Norm had come in yet.

She shook her head. "He called a little earlier to talk to you. Said he tried to get you at home, but couldn't get an answer.

Anyway, he said he wouldn't be in today, after all. He said he was going to the hospital the first thing this morning to try to see Ruth. And then he was going to drive out to Lancaster to take a couple of depositions."

"What happened last night was a real shock to him."

"I know. I feel so sorry for him...and for poor Ruth, too, of course."

Michael nodded. "It's a sad situation."

"Incidentally, Ellen called. Just a few minutes ago. She'd like you to call her sometime this morning...whenever it's convenient for you. She said she's not working today and to call her apartment."

Michael tried not to look surprised. "I'll do that," he said. He paused. "If anybody else calls, especially reporters, just say I'm not available." He started toward his office. "If Lieutenant Ferraro should call, though, I'll talk to him, of course."

He went into his office and called Ellen right away.

"Oh, Mike," she exclaimed. "I'm so glad you called. I tried to get you at your apartment, but evidently you'd already left. Anyhow, I practically had a heart attack when I heard about you and Ruth on the news this morning. Why, it's a miracle you weren't killed! The police said you had to jump off the roof of a three-story building to escape, and that you landed in a tree in a gully or something. They said you didn't hurt yourself, though. You didn't, did you, Mike?"

"Except for a few scratches and bruises, I'm just fine, Ellen."

"Oh, Mike, you could be dying, and you'd say that. I guess the only way I'll know for sure is to come over there and see for myself."

"Really, Ellen. I'm just fine."

"Well, I hope so, Mike. I was so shocked when Ruth's name was mentioned. It's still not clear to me exactly how she's mixed up in all this. The news reports weren't at all helpful. I tried a couple of different channels, and all they did was give the basic facts about capturing the kidnappers. They did say, though, that

Ruth and the girl who's Rose Queen are both all right, and that neither of them was seriously injured. They said they've both been hospitalized. Is that right?"

"Yes, they're both at Huntington Memorial Hospital."

"I'll try to get over there later today to see Ruth…that is, if she can have visitors. Do you think it will be all right, Mike?"

"Why, yes, I think so, Ellen. And I'm sure Ruth would be pleased to see you." He hesitated. "What about you? Have you managed to recover from that bad experience New Year's Eve?"

"Oh, yes." Her voice turned flat, and he could tell she didn't want to talk about it. "I'm quite all right now."

"Have you decided what you're going to do about that job offer in Washington?"

"No, I haven't. Not yet, anyhow."

"Be sure to let me know when you do, won't you, Ellen?"

"I will, Mike."

They said goodbye then, and Michael had the odd feeling that he'd just been talking to an old friend rather than to someone he'd once been married to and had thought he'd love forever. He couldn't help feeling sad about it.

He sighed and went over to the file and got out the folder on the trade infringement case that was coming up the latter part of next week. No sooner had he started to work on it than Dottie rang to tell him that Lt. Ferraro was on the phone and wanted to speak to him.

"Good morning, Mr. Donovan," the lieutenant said. "I wasn't sure you'd be working today, but I'm glad I got you. I thought you'd be interested to know what's happened since I saw you last night."

"Why, yes, I would," said Michael.

"First," the lieutenant said, "I'll give you a little rundown on that bunch of loonies we had the shootout with. That tall guy by the name of Crane, the doctor, he was seriously wounded and probably won't survive. The guy with the black beard who shot him is dead. We think he must've been trying to kill the girl and accidentally shot Crane. That's the only thing that makes any sense, anyway. The guy with the wild red hair you told us about is seriously wounded, but will probably recover. "The guy with the old-fashioned mustache you said was guarding the three of you in the bedroom closet is dead. He was riddled with bullets. The guy that was shot on the stairs of the garage died in the ambulance on the way to the hospital. None of the rest, of them—four other guys and three women—were wounded or injured. But all seven of them are in custody. You might be interested to know that one of the men is a medical doctor here in Pasadena. His name is Putnam. Ronald Putnam. Evidently he was a friend of Crane's. Can you imagine that? Two doctors involved in a harebrained effort like this?"

"The whole thing's hard to believe."

"Isn't it, though? But enough about that bunch of loonies. I thought you'd like to know that only one of our officers was wounded, and it was just a minor bullet wound in his shoulder.

"Everybody else got through unscathed. It's really a wonder we didn't have some serious casualties, considering all that heavy gunfire they put up."

"It sure is," Michael said, remembering the hail of bullets coming from the house and the garage.

"By the way, did you get to talk to your partner, Mr. Carlson, last night?"

"Yes, I did."

"Was he able to shed any light on any of this?...For instance, why his wife and that guy Conklin were kidnapped?"

"No, I'm afraid not. He's just as puzzled as I am."

"Well, I'll want to talk to him after I've talked with his wife—just to be sure I've covered all the bases."

"I'm sure he'll help in any way he can," Michael said.

"Yes, I'm sure he will. I've heard lots of good things about him."

Michael shifted the receiver to his other ear. "You mentioned Conklin. It was Conklin who introduced Mrs. Carlson to the

Cranes. I was told that Conklin used to be a professor at Cal State."

"A professor?"

"That's what I was told. He taught political science, I believe."

"Well, there wasn't a bit or identification on him. Evidently they took all his personal belongings. He didn't have a wallet or watch or keys or anything like that on him. They took everything except the clothes he was wearing. It looks as though they were planning to get rid of him...burn him up or drop his body in the ocean or something. Oh, well, it shouldn't take long to get some answers to all this. Mrs. Carlson and the girl, Carlene Edwards, should be able to clear up quite a lot of it for us. Incidentally, we dropped by the hospital this morning to talk to them, but both were scheduled for physical exams and tests, and the doctors didn't want us questioning them until this afternoon."

"Do you know whether they'll be able to have visitors then?"

"I don't know. But since they're going to let us question them, I suppose they will."

"I hope so. I'd like to see both of them."

"Well, Mr. Donovan. I've kept you much longer than I intended to. But before I let you go, I'd like to thank you once again for all your help and cooperation. I don't know whether you realize it, but you probably saved the lives of that girl and your friend by getting out of that place the way you did."

Michael was embarrassed. "I don't know about that," he said. "But it's nice of you to say so."

After they hung up, Michael got back to work on the trade infringement case. He worked right through the lunch hour and finished most of the paper work by one thirty. He stopped then, and gathered everything together and put it in the folder, and put the folder in his briefcase. Then he went out and told Dottie that he was on his way to the hospital to see Ruth and Carlene Edwards.

"Good for you, Michael." Dottie smiled approvingly. "I'm sure they'll be glad to see you." She paused. "Be sure to give Ruth my love, and tell her Bill and I will drop by this evening to see her."

"I'll do that, Dottie." He shook his finger at her with a look of mock sternness. "But now I want you to stop what you're doing, close up the office, and take the rest of the day off. You've been working far too hard these past few weeks."

"*Leave now*?" She indicated the stacks of papers and folders on her desk. "You must be joking, Michael."

"No, I'm not. I couldn't be more serious."

"But. Michael, I—"

"Come on, now, Dottie.. Whatever you're working on can be put off at least a couple of days, or even longer."

She hesitated, her eyes crinkling with thought. "You know," she said, "I could go get Bill and we could go to the mall. It would do him a world of good to get away from that store for a while."

"I'm sure it would," he smiled.

"All right, Michael." She smiled back at him. "You've got yourself a deal." She looked at her watch. "Give me a minute or two to put these things away, and I'll walk out with you."

Chapter 37

MICHAEL STOPPED BY THE HOSPITAL gift shop and got a pot of yellow chrysanthemums for Ruth. He thought they would brighten up her room, and he knew she'd probably plant them in her backyard when she got home, the way she usually did with gifts of plants and flowers.

Her room was on the second floor, three doors down from the elevators. She got a bit tearful when she saw the chrysanthemums he'd brought her.

"Oh, Mike, how sweet of you! They're lovely." She gestured toward a little table in the corner. "If you like, you can put them over there."

Michael set the chrysanthemums on the table, then turned back to her. In the light from the windows, her face looked less bruised and swollen than it had last night.

She gave him a sad little smile. "Thanks, Mike."

"You're welcome, Ruth." He paused. "How're you feeling? Is your knee any better?"

"Oh, I'm all right, I guess. But my knee isn't. They're going to have to operate on it. I'll probably be here several more days."

"Sorry about that, Ruth."

She pointed at the nearest chair. "Sit down, Mike."

He sat down and looked at her sympathetically. "You've had a pretty rough time of it, haven't you?"

She shrugged. "It could've been worse." Her voice trembled a bit. "I'll never be able to repay you for what you did last night, Mike. Those horrible creatures would never've let us stay alive after they killed Fred, you know."

"I guess we were pretty lucky to make it out of there."

"We wouldn't have, if it hadn't been for you. The police were here right after lunch to question me, and they gave me all the particulars about what happened."

It made him uncomfortable to talk about himself. "Have you heard from Norm?"

Her expression turned rueful. "Yes, he was here early this morning and left me a note and those lovely red carnations." She nodded at the vase of flowers on the windowsill. "I was still asleep when he got here...the nurse had given me a strong sedative, I guess...so I didn't get to talk to him." Her eyes started to fill with tears. "His note said he had to go to Lancaster to take some depositions, and that he'd see me this evening when he got back." She brushed at her tears. "Dear, sweet Norm. Always thinking of the welfare of others rather than himself."

Michael nodded. "He's been very worried about you, Ruth. After they put you in the ambulance last night, I dropped by to tell Norm what happened. He was still up waiting for you to come home."

Her eyes started to till with tears again. "Sorry, Mike," she said in a husky voice. "I'm having an awful time dealing with my emotions today." She pulled a piece of tissue paper from the box on the table beside her and dabbed at her eyes.

"You've been through quite an ordeal, Ruth. It's no wonder you feel the way you do."

She cleared her throat. "Have you learned yet how I got involved in this awful mess?"

He shook his head. "No. I haven't."

"Has Norm?"

"I don't think so. He hadn't when I left him late last night anyway."

"Well, if you have the time, Mike and you don't mind, I'd like to talk to you about it. I've been carrying this guilt around with me for a long time now, and it'll do me a lot of good to get it off my chest."

"I'll be glad to listen. Take as long as you like, Ruth. I've got plenty of time."

She cleared her throat again. "It...it all goes back well over a year ago. I met Fred Conklin at a seminar at Cal State. He'd been teaching political science there for a number of years. I was impressed by how bright and knowledgeable he was, but I was even more impressed by how sensitive and well-read he was. During the next few months we'd get together every now and then for coffee and to talk about teaching and politics and literature and all kinds of things. We did it quite innocently and openly at first, meeting in public places. But it wasn't long until we realized we were beginning to care for each other in a special way. It wasn't too big a problem for Fred, because he'd been divorced for a couple of years, although he did feel guilty because of my being married. It was a huge problem for me though, because I do love Norm. I know it's a cliche, but it is possible to love two persons at the same time. I can certainly testify to that." She shrugged and gave Michael a sad little smile.

"Anyhow," she continued, "after Fred and I realized how we felt about each other, he confided in me that he was working undercover for the government in investigating extreme right-wing movements spreading through the country. He told me that he and a couple of other men who'd been recruited along with him had already infiltrated the Southern California branch of White Unity." She paused and shook her head. "Sounds incredible, doesn't it?"

He nodded. "These are strange times, Ruth."

She grimaced. "Isn't that the truth? Well, anyhow, to get on with this, I guess it was inevitable that I'd get involved in what

Fred was doing, what with our seeing each other as often as we did. One weekend when Norm was staying over on a case in San Francisco, Fred and I flew to Las Vegas, just to get away from everything. I'm afraid we weren't very discreet, and we shared a room at the Hilton. Ironically, the first evening we were there we ran into Albert Crane and his wife just as we were leaving our room. It was very awkward for us, but it didn't seem to faze them at all. They seemed delighted to see us, and asked us to join them for drinks and for dinner. And we did. After that, they assumed that I shared the views that Fred professed to have, and they regarded me as one of them. Of course, Fred didn't want me involved at all, but there wasn't much he could do about it."

"So Norm had no idea you were involved with Conklin all this time? Or what Conklin was up to?"

"Oh, no. Absolutely not."

"But what about Albert Crane? How did a medical doctor, a highly educated man like him, fit into this crazy movement? He seemed very smart and sophisticated when I met him at your party."

"Oh, he's smart and sophisticated, all right. He came here from Miami, Florida, where apparently he'd had a very successful practice in internal medicine. I understand, though, that he got involved in radical right-wing activities there, and seriously damaged his standing in the medical community. So that's why he came out here. And he hadn't been here very long, I guess, before he got several doctors in this area who were adamantly opposed to socialized medicine in any form to join him in his effort to stop it. One of the doctors was Ronald Putnam, a well-known orthopedic surgeon here in Pasadena. Maybe you know him, Mike."

Michael's stomach tightened. "He testified briefly in a case I was involved in last summer, but I really don't know him." He decided it was pointless to tell her anything more than that.

"Well," she said, "to get back to Albert Crane, he and his

doctor friends got involved with the White Unity movement. I don't think they really endorsed many of the things the movement stood for, but they cynically used it as a means to accomplish their own goals or agenda. At least that's what Fred thought. He thought Crane was brilliant, but a borderline psychotic. He said Crane was willing to do almost anything to stop the move toward socialized medicine and the socialization of our federal government."

"Was it Crane's idea to kidnap Carlene Edwards?"

She nodded. "He insisted it would be an easy way to pick up a large amount of money, as well as publicize the goals of White Unity on a national scale."

"And I suppose it was also his idea to firebomb her home."

"Yes, it was. He said it would create lots of fear and turmoil, and they'd be able to exploit it in a number of ways that would benefit the White Unity movement."

Michael shook his head. "How did Crane and the others finally get wise to you and your friend Fred Conklin?"

"I really don't know, Mike, but I suppose it was the result of several things. I think they first became suspicious when Fred tried to talk them out of kidnapping Carlene Edwards. And then, later, I guess they became even more suspicious when he objected to their plan to firebomb Carlene's home. In fact, we thought he'd talked them out of it but they went ahead and did it anyway."

Michael frowned. "It must've been awfully scary to you to see how depraved they actually were, how cunning and manipulative."

"Oh, it was. We didn't know what to expect next. After they abducted Fred and me last night, they told us they'd put a tap on our telephones and recorded all our conversations over the past two weeks. And even though we were always very careful about what we said when we talked to each other, they evidently learned enough to confirm their suspicions about us."

"But when and how did they manage to kidnap you?"

"Oh, that was quite easy for them, I guess. Norm and I were supposed to go to a party a teacher friend of mine was having after the football game yesterday. Norm didn't feel up to it though and insisted I go alone. Instead, I called Fred from a pay phone and arranged to meet him at his apartment. I hadn't been there more than a few minutes when Crane's lackeys came bursting in, grabbed us, and took us up to that place in the hills above the Rose Bowl."

Michael leaned back in the chair, eying her with a mixture of sympathy and curiosity.

"Here's something else that's puzzled me, Ruth. What about Norm's guns? Who came up with the idea of stealing them? Was that Crane's idea, too?"

She looked regretful. "Yes, it was. I was very foolish and invited Fred and the Cranes over for dinner a few weeks ago. I guess maybe I wanted to see Fred and Norm together to make comparisons, to see which one...Oh, I don't know. It was stupid of me, really. Anyhow, Norm, as usual, had to show his guns to the men, and I guess Crane decided he could use some of them. Not long after that, he had a couple of his men break in and steal them. I didn't learn about it until afterwards of course."

She adjusted the pillows behind her back and looked across at him, her eyes sad and troubled.

"I've really made a terrible mess of everything, haven't I, Mike? If only I'd never met Fred...if only..." She frowned. "Do you think Norm can ever forgive me?"

Chapter 38

He said goodbye to Ruth, then went back down to the gift shop on the first floor to get something for Carlene Edwards. He selected a dozen long-stemmed American Beauty roses, and then went up to Carlene's room, which was also on the second floor.

Carlene's eyes widened in disbelief when he stepped into the room.

"Why, Mr. Donovan," she exclaimed. "What a nice surprise!"

"Hello, Carlene," he said, smiling. He indicated the roses he was carrying. "These are for you."

Her eyes filled with tears. "Why, they're beautiful. You really shouldn't have, Mr. Donovan."

"I don't see why not," he said. "After all, you are the Queen of Roses, aren't you?"

She tried to smile. "Well, it's very nice of you," she said. Her voice turned husky. "I thank you with all my heart."

"Want me to put them on the table there?"

"Would you, please?"

He put the roses near the end of the table so it would be easy for her to see them from her bed.

"Please sit down, Mr. Donovan. I still can't get over your coming to see me."

He smiled and sat down on the chair nearest to her. "I'm just one of thousands who've been worried about you, Carlene."

Her eyes started to fill with tears again. "I want to thank you for all you've done for me," she said, wiping her eyes with her fingers. "My sister, Clarice, was here only a few minutes ago, and she told me how brave you were. She said it was on all the TV stations, and in the paper, and everyone was talking about it."

Michael felt a surge of admiration for her. Except for the bandage on the side of her head and the bruises on her cheeks and neck, you'd never guess what she'd been through for the past few days.

"I want to compliment you for the way you're handling all this," he said. "You're a remarkable person, Carlene. We're all proud of you."

She started to speak, then stopped, obviously moved.

"Have you thought about what you're going to do when you get out of here?" he asked.

She hesitated. "The doctors said I could check out tomorrow morning, and an elderly neighbor of ours has asked me to stay with her. She's very nice, and all alone, and I think it will be good for both of us."

"You'll go on to school, won't you?"

"Oh, yes. Nothing can stop me from doing that. I'll finish out the year at Pasadena City College, and then transfer to USC in the fall. I was very lucky and got a full-time scholarship there."

"Well, congratulations! That's wonderful. Have you decided what you're going to major in, what you'd like to do when you graduate?"

She nodded with a shy smile. "I'd like to do just what you're doing. I'd like to practice law. And I'd like to specialize in civil rights law."

"Good for you," he said. "It's a very important part of our judicial system. I think you'll make a fine lawyer."

"Thank you, Mr. Donovan."

"You're welcome," he said. "If there's anything I can do to help you, I want you to let me know. Nothing would please me more than to see you accomplish your goals." He glanced at his watch. "I think I'd better go now. I have some work I have to finish this afternoon." He got to his feet.

"Thank you for coming," she said. Her voice was husky with emotion again. "And thank you for the beautiful roses."

"It's my pleasure, Carlene. Remember, now, I want you to keep in touch with me."

"Oh, I will, Mr. Donovan. I promise. And thank you again for all you did for me. I'll never forget you or your kindness."

Chapter 39

Dottie was gone when he got back to his office. He smiled to himself, glad she had taken the rest of the day off.

As he started to take the trade infringement folder out of his briefcase, the phone rang. It was Jan Ashby.

"Mike?"

He got a sudden warm feeling inside. "Hi, Jan. You can't guess how glad I am to hear your voice."

"Well, you can't guess how glad I am to hear yours," she said. "I could hardly believe what I heard on the news about you and Ruth and that girl who's Rose Queen. I was so relieved to hear you weren't hurt. You could've been killed, Mike."

"Guess I'm just lucky, Jan."

"Evidently Ruth and the girl are all right, too, aren't they?"

"Yes, they're just fine, considering what they've been through. In fact, I just got back from visiting them in the hospital. Ruth hurt her knee, and will have to have it operated on. Otherwise, though, she's all right. And the girl is all right, too, except for some bruises and abrasions."

"Well, that's good to hear. I would've called earlier, but I was down at Newport Beach with those friends of Mother's I told you about. We were out on their boat until around two, so I didn't hear the news until we came in. I came right home then to try to get in touch with you." She paused. "I'm not working tonight, Mike, and I'd love to see you. Do you think we could get together?"

"Why, yes," he said, pleased at the thought of seeing her. "I'd like to."

"Wonderful," she said. "We'll do something special to celebrate your getting safely away from those horrible men and saving Ruth and that girl. You're quite a hero, Mike. I'm so proud of you!"

"Really, Jan. I'm anything but a hero."

"Now, Mike. I know better. So to celebrate, I'm going to treat you to a sumptuous dinner at the Carlton House. And if you feel like talking about what happened last night, I'll be glad to listen. And if you don't, why, we'll talk about whatever you feel like talking about."

"Sounds wonderful, Jan."

"I can meet you there any time you like. Or pick you up at your apartment. Which do you prefer?"

"Why don't we just meet there? It'll be easier for you."

"Fine. What's a good time for you? Six or seven? Or even later, if you like."

"The sooner, the better," he said. "I can't wait to see you. I've been thinking of you all day." And it was true. Even as busy as he'd been, he'd been thinking of her since the moment he got up that morning.

"Oh, Mike," she cried. "I absolutely adore you!"

He got to the Carlton House at exactly six o'clock, and Jan was already there, sitting in an armchair in the lobby waiting for him.

When she saw him, she got quickly to her feet to greet him. She was wearing an attractive white dress, and her blonde hair, bleached almost white from the sun, was drawn back from her forehead and tied with a black velvet ribbon at the back of her neck.

She looked slim and golden and beautiful, and she was smiling at him in a very warm and loving way.

Printed in the United States
45697LVS00006B/154-204